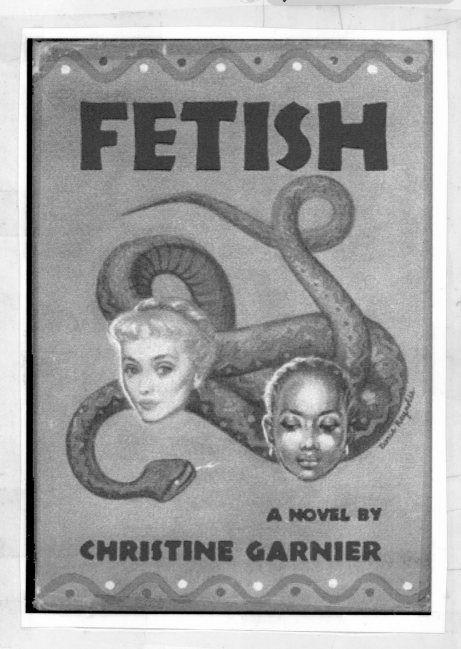

FETISH

A NOVEL BY

CHRISTINE GARNIER

FETISH

Christine Garnier

FETISH

TRANSLATED BY NAOMI WALFORD

G. P. Putnam's Sons   New York

To

J.-B. FRALON

FETISH

1

Boko ke kà nu be ahua le gbea ji a Boko
a nito myàl ahua me.

(The soothsayer who foretold war finds
himself involved in the conflict.)

MY NAME is Doéllé.

My grandfather, who bestowed on my family the
name of D'Almeiga, traded slaves along the coast of
Africa from Cape Verde to the Gulf of Benin. He was
the son of a Portuguese of good family with a thirst for
adventure, and of a girl of the Ewe tribe; no doubt it is
to him that I owe my aristocratic nose, and my skin that
is more golden than black. Yet my mother, a Mina of
Accra, was born with the broad toes of a race that has
never worn sandals. Look, my toes are like that too. And
it's not from choice that I dress my hair in the Abongo
fashion, with my scalp divided into neat rectangles and
the end of each lock flattened and greased and tied with

3

black thread. I prefer European styles, but alas, my hair is too fuzzy to conform to them.

People say I'm beautiful. Sometimes white women have wanted to give me their frocks, but I always refused them. I don't want to dress like other Europeanized Africans, in short, tight clothes, and I wear the lovely Gold Coast blankets that hide the ankles and leave the shoulders bare.

I'm a nurse at the maternity clinic. Thanks to my Catholic education and my studies in Dakar, the white people of Manoho never address me as *tu*. Sometimes they even say *Mademoiselle*. They pretend to have forgotten that my mother regularly takes offerings to the Temple of Pythons and that my sister Océa lately met a shameful death at the hands of pagan priests. White people smile at me; yet they well know me to have been rootless and nationless since the lure of their civilization turned me from my path. They know that while I'm being dragged forward into the future I still clutch at the meshes of an ancient, outworn way of life. But what is that to them? They drag me ever faster, ever more irresistibly along their road, jostling what is left in me of ancestral quiet, overlaying my thoughts with theirs. White people talk to me politely. But when they have no further use for me they say, "Thank you, Doéllé, you may go." And their wave of farewell means: "Go back now, Doéllé, to your place among the Africans. Your skin is soft but your lips are thick and your hips jut out too sharply. You're not one of us. Go to your own people."

4

THIS was how it began.

One December morning I was standing on the threshold of the maternity clinic, slowly buttoning a white overall over my robe and looking at the lagoon. The coconut palms were already yellow from the drought and drooped their weary fronds. Along the red, winding road, bare-breasted women were walking in profile like figures in a fresco. Near the hospital, patients lay about on the ground propped on one elbow, chin in hand, staring at the lagoon as if it looked somehow different today.

5

And surely it was, very different.

The torpor pervading the pale sky and the pale sea, the stillness about the walking women and prostrate men —these were nothing new. It was the quiet. Not a laugh was to be heard, not even a sigh. The golden-yellow weaverbirds that usually flitted among the *filaos* were not singing. The lagoon lay ringed in silence and said to me softly, "Wait . . . wait . . . listen!" It seemed to say, "Be careful, Doéllé. Difficult days are coming."

For the lagoon, like crossroads and fetish groves, is as much alive as you or I: it speaks to those who can hear. One has but to listen and rightly interpret its message; to answer with respect; to treat it not as a common, stagnant pool, but rather as an invisible power that can bring happiness or unleash evil according to its mood. That day the lagoon gave me a warning, and I was uneasy as I stood there chewing a twig of *allo* to whiten my teeth.

"*Eso bedo*, Doéllé!"

The old women in the faded robes who brought water to the patients were greeting me in the Mina language. They spoke in low voices so as not to vex the lagoon or break the enchanted stillness. And the women who sold salt, smoked mudfish and potash soap—all these women who had known me as a child in my mother's hut—whispered too: "*Eso bedo*, Doéllé."

The everyday words began all at once to bring pictures to my mind; they took on a new value. White people, translating them by a commonplace "Good day," are ignorant of their meaning, which is "Thank you for yesterday." Thank you for my life yesterday. . . .

"*Eso bedo!*" I exclaimed silently to the lagoon. For yesterday was beautiful. I am happy and my love is sweet. It is as if I should never die, on this clockless coast where even white people discard their watches. Not one of the forty dialects spoken here has terms to denote hours, months or years, or passing youth. Why think, brood, ponder or make plans? I don't want to fight against life, I want to let it flow like cornmeal through my fingers.

It seemed to me then that the lagoon smothered a sad little laugh, but I no longer heeded it. For the heavy silence that so oppressed me was over. In the doctor's bungalow, behind lowered *sekos*, could be heard for the first time for two years the light step of a woman.

Of this European wife, who the day before had stepped off the boat from France, I knew nothing. Often during my bush treks with the doctor, on the trail of yaws and leprosy, I thought he might tell me of her. The evenings passed so slowly and we were so much alone. But Capitaine Docteur, reserved as any African, had not so much as pronounced her name. The only hint of his love for her was betrayed by the trembling of his hands when the weekly mail from France arrived. His austere face remained impassive, double-locked, but his fingers would suddenly come alive and tap out imaginary scales if the boy was late in returning from the post; or he would clench his fists until the knuckles whitened if the boy said, "Nothing, Capitaine Docteur."

Then there was the quick flushing and paling of his face as he read the letter. Fearing on her account the sticky dampness of Manoho he would not let her join him there until nearly the end of his stay, so that they might sail together after only a few months. And here she was! So keen was my curiosity that I forgot the warnings of the lagoon. What manner of woman had the blessed good fortune to be the wife of the man I so deeply respected?

In my impatience I too began nervously tapping the worm-eaten wood of the railing.

At last a dimly seen figure raised one of the *sekos*, those shutters of interlaced strips of bamboo, and in a voice which at that distance sounded to me rather pathetic she cried, "Oh, Frantz, the lagoon's much lovelier than you described it!"

"Is it?" said the doctor in surprise. "I've looked at it for eighteen months and now I just don't notice it."

"It's queer, but I feel as if I'd been here before," she went on. "I seem to know those yellowish coconut palms and the water without any reflections and the women walking along the red road. I know the lagoon too. I must have been here in some former life."

"You'll get on well with the natives," returned the doctor. "They live in a dream-world too, and they have a passion for dragging the supernatural into the most everyday affairs. With them the possible and the impossible, wish and fact, poetry and thought, knowledge

8

and belief, visible and invisible are all mixed up. You'll find that out for yourself."

As this conversation was carried on in the shadow of the *seko* I still had not glimpsed the face of the newcomer; yet already I sensed that these two did not understand one another. Probably the doctor, in loving his wife, loved some other woman in her; and she must have felt very lonely with her husband.

Unable any longer to restrain my impatience I ran over to their bungalow. My pretext was a natural one: I would ask for the key of the dispensary.

I clapped my hands loudly, twice, as do all callers at these doorless dwellings, and the doctor appeared at the top of the wooden steps, wearing a long white overall over his shorts. His shoulders were sturdy as ever, his flesh hard and firm as cement. Childishly I had feared that the coming of Madame Docteur might have changed him into someone else.

"*Eso bedo*, Doctor. I wanted some sulphonamides for the miscarriage case in Hut Five. She's in a high fever."

"Doéllé! Come on up."

He smiled. I noticed that notwithstanding the trying climate his cheeks were fresh-colored as fruit—one would have liked to bite them if one had dared. He half-turned toward the veranda and in a voice that seemed neither more nor less gentle he called, "Urgèle!"

So I learned her name; then, beneath the ornamental plants on the veranda—those broad leaves patched with vermilion and known as painter's palettes—I saw her coming.

9

She looked like the lagoon. Yes, that was it! Artless yet golden, simple yet radiant, burning yet remote; two faces, two contradictory aspects, and yet . . . That morning, ill at ease with me, she was not sure whether to offer me her hand. No doubt in Paris people had said to her: "Don't treat the natives too familiarly—especially the *évolués*.* They understand and obey strength and admire disdain. Treat them rough if you want to be respected." She looked at me hesitantly, as she must have looked yesterday at the native nursing orderlies who ran to her with the bouquet of welcome: hibiscus and frangipani.

"You remember—I told you about her in my letters," the doctor persisted. "Doéllé's my best nurse. She's your age—twenty-seven. I think you'll enjoy listening to all her stories about fetishes and amulets and the blood pact. Doéllé knows everything about the customs of her country; I'm always telling her she should write a book —aren't I, Doéllé?"

We smiled, all three of us. Yes, at that time, incredible as it may seem, we could still smile.

The seas breaking against the bar sent their foaming, booming sound into the big, sparsely furnished rooms that looked out over the sea. Calm voices near the hospital made background music to the shrill laughter of the boys, Bokari and Kankwe, who were preparing breakfast.

"What's the name of that big gray tree?" asked

* *évolué*: literate or Europeanized African.

10

Urgèle in her grave voice, her arm stretched out toward the lagoon.

"It's a baobab," said the doctor.

"That one's a sacred baobab," I put in. "In the daytime it looks like any other baobab, doesn't it? But at night it puts on a white robe and wanders through Manoho choosing who shall die next."

"Rather gloomy," added the doctor. "You'd better look at the coconut palms instead, Urgèle; they're not so grim."

At his order the boy left the lemons he was squeezing, ran swiftly to the top of the tallest coconut and, having thrown its green fruit to the ground, came down again like a monkey. I remember that Madame Docteur found the milk warm and sickly.

"You'll get used to it," the doctor assured her in his precise tones. "In the bush it's the most natural kind of filtered water. After a day of pirogues, lepers, alligators and hippopotamus you'll be crying out for the drink you despise today. Unless you think these treks will be too tiring for you, and you'd rather stay at home? I warned you, Urgèle, we don't lead a drawing-room life here."

Without seeing the look of reproach she gave him he swung round on his heel: a powerful figure, seemingly carved from rock. At the foot of the steps a native assistant was waiting for him and together they walked away to the hospital, leaving me alone with Urgèle who was still holding the glass of coconut milk; could I ever have imagined what trouble was to be brought upon the house by this same liquid?

The trusty arrived, dragging his feet, and, bending over a tiny broom, he began sweeping the floor of the veranda. He was an albino: his black skin was patched with pink and his eyes were reddish, giving him so repellent an appearance that Madame Docteur recoiled.

"Don't be afraid, Madame Docteur," I said. "It's only Kanjo. The name means Monday, for among the Ajigos children are called after the day of their birth. We say here that albinos are children of the moon, and my sister Océa believes that they're dead people who've come back. But here's Amalia the mulatto, who'll be doing your needlework for you."

Slowly, majestically and with a disdainful air, Amalia after a brief smile seated herself on the veranda by a raised *seko* and began to hem a cloth. She was proud of the light skin and pale Germanic eyes that she had inherited from one of our early colonists. Like me she had been brought up by the Mission Sisters, and became a dressmaker. But to work for white people was for her a fiery and humiliating trial. Every five minutes she would lay down her work and, leaning on her elbows beneath the raised *seko*, gaze fixedly at the lagoon.

Meanwhile Madame Docteur had taken me to her room that overlooked the sea. The familiar house saddened me: for a moment I hardly knew it. The dwelling of a man living alone is nearly always impersonal and can arouse no painful feelings. No memories jump out at you; there are no flowers—nothing to evoke other presences. But with the advent of a woman everything springs to life; reticences, things unsaid, clutch at the heart. The ebony sculptures from the Cameroons were still in their place, certainly, as were the broad-striped Sudanese blankets and the elephant tusk. But suitcases gaped on the floor, heavy with unknown fragrance. Silk and velvet dresses spread their folds across the faded cotton covers of the chairs. To match the Konkomba helmet, dangling its ropes of cowrie shells down the wall hung a sun helmet, the trimmest and smallest I had ever seen. Among the Dahomey carvings Parisian necklaces, like stiff serpents, were entwined.

In the presence of this foreigner, who was already dabbing her streaming forehead before the heat of the day had begun, I stood discomfited; for the world that she had brought with her in her luggage I should never know. I breathed the perfumes, I heard the crisp rustle of taffeta, my finger followed the curve of a silver shoe, but within me rang the voice of the white man—the frowning white man: "Don't touch, Doéllé! Why should you? None of this is for you—yet. Be patient. Later, perhaps—"

Learning the ways of white men is not enough; speaking their language and reading their books is not enough. There are doors that they keep carefully shut and will open only to our children—perhaps, indeed, only to our grandchildren. Unless they keep the magic key to themselves forever? And the old misery that I sought constantly to fly from, born of the burning conflict between two civilizations, assailed me again as I stood there with open hands before the lace underclothes and the hair nets starred with gold. I felt disconcerted, off balance, unsatisfied, like a girl whose lover had long caressed without possessing her, and sends her away saying, "That'll do for today."

Meanwhile Madame Docteur, attracted by singing from the road, had once more hastened onto the veranda whither I followed her, glad to escape from that baleful room. A procession of fetish priestesses was passing on its way to the Temple of the Sea. The devotees shook their rattles and moved their shoulders like wings; their bodies were anointed with palm oil and their loins swathed in white robes.

"Tell me," Madame Docteur was saying, "who are they and where are they going? Are they really fetishers? And you, Doéllé—do you believe in fetishes?"

"Oh no, Madame! I love God—I despise fetishes. When I meet a fetisher I look up to heaven, and when a demon attacks me I make the sign of the cross."

"But that must annoy the fetishers?"

"They hate me because I don't give them any money. When my sister Océa is pleased with one of their *grigris* —amulets—she gives them joints of meat and robes from the Gold Coast. As for my mother—! One day my mother was ill; she said an enemy had bewitched her with the skin of a chameleon chopped up in her food. The witch doctor came to our hut. I was quite small but I remember it. He wore a necklace of glass beads and

14

ostrich-egg shells, and he looked into the eyes of all the women there. He leaped and danced and sang more and more frantically, and at last he put his mouth to my mother's chest to draw out the sickness. My mother swears that everyone there saw a hideous chameleon dart from her right breast and escape into the bush. From that day she was cured, and she was so grateful that she gave the witch doctor all her ornaments."

"If all the natives of Manoho are as generous, the fetishers must be very rich," remarked Madame Docteur.

"No indeed!" I exclaimed with warmth—whether sincere or affected I hardly knew. "No one can prosper without God in his hut. And when the hut's untidy and full of dirt, God can't come in."

"What a good Christian you are, Doéllé!" cried Madame Docteur, with a deep little laugh. I had talked to her so naturally that she could never guess at the sorrow and pain inflicted on me by that scented room. She went on laughing and looking at me with narrowed eyes, as if slightly doubting my love for the God of the Catholics. Certainly she never suspected that I had already begun to hate her.

I was jealous of her for being white and for belonging so completely to the beguiling world that lay just beyond my reach. I was jealous of her beauty.

I didn't know then that she could cast spells to crack the husk of a man, tear the mask from his heart, and lay bare his secrets. I didn't know that she was a white witch, more to be feared than the novices who shook their rattles along the road, far more dangerous than the dulled, flabby, toothless fetish women who had been amassing supernatural powers throughout their lives. On that first day I noticed only her beauty. It was her fair hair, her rather green eyes, and her grace that confirmed me in my discomfiture and hatred.

A pity, I thought. Really a great pity. That pink-icing freshness can't last. Soon the harmattan—the seasonal wind that from January to March careers across the desert to the ocean—will be blowing, irritating throats, skins, and nerves with its parching breath. It will bring explosions: all kinds of jealousy, anger, and madness, and one morning Madame Docteur, gazing into the mirror that's spotted with drops from the shower, won't recognize herself; there'll be no color in her cheeks, but her eyelids will have a bluish tinge— no sparkle in her eyes, but a line at each side of her mouth. It's true there are a few weeks to go; till then you'll clap your hands at the agile Yaya as he climbs the coconut palm, you'll say that African women have the most beautiful shoulders in the world, and the scent of frangipani will seem to you exquisite. Wait, Madame Docteur, wait. . . . Gradually your gowns will begin to rot. A green and white furry mildew will lay siege to your shoes, bags, and leather belts. And when prickly heat has speckled your bosom and wrists you'll begin to see that this is no place for you; that here, for a white woman accustomed to silks and soft lights, all is menace: the sun that pierces eyes and neck, the humidity that at night freezes the lungs, the water, the mosquitoes—

16

everything, Madame Docteur. And not only your beauty is threatened, or your health. There is also your self-assurance, the insolent poise of the white woman who steps off the boat from France as if saying, "The others who were here before me couldn't stand it, but with me it'll be different." Wait, wait, Madame Docteur! The rolling boom of waters against the bar will drive you mad. Day and night the pitiless regularity of that sound . . . You fancy that your intelligence and education will protect you from boredom? That you will study native customs and reactions? But of these Fons, Minas, Hausar, Kotokolis—of all these heterogeneous groups formed here at the tail end of a migration—you can learn nothing clear or true. We don't confide in foreigners, Madame Docteur. We're silent, or we lie.

Meanwhile the morning wore on. In a polite tone that concealed the rage in my heart I instructed Madame Docteur in the everyday details of colonial life.

"Never take a cold shower," I advised her, "because of blackwater fever. A white woman at this station— the District Officer's wife—had it and has never quite recovered. Kanjo will bring hot water to your bathroom every morning. For cleaning your teeth there's filtered water in the refrigerator: that's to avoid dysentery and Guinea worm. . . ."

A young Ashanti girl with a sparkling smile, carrying a basin on her head, came to sell fish. I stopped Madame Docteur, who was already holding out the money.

"Never pay what they ask, Madame Docteur! It's always too much. And to that boy you must never give any money: the vegetables he brings you are from the District Officer's garden."

Madame Docteur thanked me each time with a smile, glad to feel supported, protected, and guided in what was to her the labyrinth of a new life. But I kept thinking: "How bored you'll be, Madame Docteur! Twenty days out of thirty your husband will be in the bush and for the most part you won't be able to go with him. What will you do with yourself all alone in the bungalow? One can't always be writing letters, choosing cotton stuffs in the market, or reading and sleeping. And so? Wandering round and round these empty rooms with nothing to do—unwell, anxious without cause—you'll turn in upon your conscience. You'll brood over yourself, study the attitude of the eight or nine white people in the station, analyze every word of the letters you get, worry, ask yourself questions, build dreams and weep. . . . I have watched other white women. They arrive bright-eyed. They gaze, marveling, at the lagoon, as you did—and soon they put on dark glasses to escape the sight of it."

"Au revoir, Doéllé," Madame Docteur was saying as she dabbed her forehead with a little green handkerchief. "Au revoir and thank you. I shall be all at sea at first in these new surroundings, and you must be my guardian angel."

I was already going down the steps when she held out to me a bottle of the alien and disturbing scent that hung about the suitcases in her room. I reflected that Flavien might like the smell and that at Christmas I would sprinkle some on my new robe so as to be even more attractive to him. Amalia, leaning on her elbows, withdrew her gaze from the lagoon and followed me with her pale, German eyes. We had been friends once, at the Sisters'; but since then, regarding my position as superior to hers, she had been growing jealous. She was now furious because I had talked so long with Madame Docteur—furious above all because I'd been given the bottle of scent.

At the maternity clinic people were wondering at my long absence. Amavi, the second nurse, had attended to the six confinement cases, and she was just talking to me about the miscarriage case in Hut Five, who had a high temperature, when a truck drew up before us in a cloud of red dust. A family emerged from it, powdered with the same red dust and carrying cans of oil, a pitcher of drinking water, and a cloth decorated with a pattern of birds for one of the maternity cases. They rushed toward us shouting joyfully, as was the custom, "*Tohun, tohun!* The ear is open!" They meant that the event had turned out well.

Leaving Amavi and the midwives amid the clamor I drove the medical van to Voagnan, one of the fifteen bush dispensaries that I had to visit each month. I drove quickly, with throbbing temples.

"Let's see, there are the babies to be examined—yes, and they've all got malaria—constant reinfection from bites—infant mortality high. . . . Pregnant women come less and less often for consultation—they prefer fetishers to nurses, the insides of cockroaches to sulpha drugs, and the course of nature to the stethoscope. Yes, it's a bore, but that's not what's on my mind. *What is that Urgèle doing among us?*"

The laterite road ran beneath the tires, dust falling back upon the drooping palm fronds like a rain of blood. As a rule I loved the intoxication of speed, the corrugations of the road, the sculptured waves of the wheel ruts and the half-ruinous timber bridges. I loved the dry splash of tall grasses against the wind screen; I liked stripping away lianas, crushing anthills, and tearing bushes. It did me good. But that day I saw nothing: neither the fan palms against the sky, nor the palm rats darting to shelter beneath the maize. I was following the path of my cares.

"What a fine place Africa would be for the white man, if only he wouldn't bring the white woman with him! He can stand the climate much better than she can. His work interests him and gives him a sense of freedom —illusory, perhaps, but heady. The doctor driving his mobile clinic from village to remote village, the police officer investigating the poisoning of a king, the agricultural officer counting his manioc plants, the D.O. absorbed in his palavers, the engineer in his bridges, the cassava planter in his crops. They're busy, they get about, they feel useful; they feel they're leaving their mark. But the wives! Happy the husband who resists the temptation of bringing his wife out here! Happy he who submits unmoved to torrents of reproach! Madame Docteur, I won't have you worrying and annoying Capitaine Docteur; he, more than anyone, needs peace. His work is hard. When he's in the bush tracking down disease, drinking tepid drinks, and sleeping under the stars in his narrow camp bed, he is, after nightfall, a prey to solitude. He can't read because of the mosquitoes that swarm about the carbide lamp. He must be able to keep smoking his pipe up to the borders of sleep without tormenting himself with thoughts of emotional upsets. When he comes back to your bungalow, eager to take a shower, open the icebox and read his mail, it won't be to stay at your side, Madame Docteur. Patients await him at the hospital; there are operations to perform in a scorching little room where instruments rust and rubber rots, where drugs soften and turn moldy. Having inspected meat and carried out autopsies on three suspect bodies, he'll see to the lunatics who yell and sob amid the foul stench of their excrements. Every school in the Manoho area is looking out for him: the pupils bare their shoulder blades and open innumerable mouths before him—to say nothing of the white people, these few at the station who worry and fidget when he's away, who are panic-stricken at the most trivial disorder, and who, the moment he returns, rush at him with endless stories of their headaches and temperatures. No, Madame Docteur, your husband will have no time to attend to you. You'd better make up your mind to that at once."

Inhabitants of the surrounding villages were moving in long files on their way to market, bearing on their heads bunches of bananas, kids with bound feet, precarious erections of calabashes, jars of palm wine, clucking hens and pyramids of pineapples. Scared by the speed of the medical truck, they scattered into the tall grass of the roadside whence only their black heads could be seen, surmounted by their loads. Dust veiled them in a red cloud. One of my hands left the steering wheel to give a friendly wave, but they barely acknowledged it. By them, alas, I am regarded as a "false, bold woman, not to be trusted: she likes the whites too much."

But how do I seem to the whites? A rootless creature whom they keep at a careful distance from their social gatherings and their interests. When will they forget that my skin is black, or I that theirs is white? During our bush treks Capitaine Docteur would talk to me of these weighty problems to which no solution has yet been found.

"Doéllé," he would say, "for more than a hundred years Africans and Europeans have been in contact, and yet even now we know very little of each other. You need our dynamic nature, our knowledge, and leadership—but it's your hands that build the roads and bridges, it's you who labor in the plantations and iron mines. In these spheres we complement each other fairly harmoniously. On the emotional plane it's different. The white man, being ignorant of your language, can't grasp the complexity of the native character, and he takes too small a part in your daily life to be interested in your little troubles. And you no doubt blame us for building new things and failing to base them on the solid foundations of the old. And that's only part of it . . ."

Capitaine Docteur understands it all. Capitaine Docteur is patience, tenacity, and courage. "*Enyé Amé*" is what they say of him in Manoho: "He's a man." For me he was a rocklike figure. Yet as I drew up at the round, lime-washed huts of the dispensary I had a painful foreboding that this statue would soon topple from its pedestal and be smashed.

Women, crouching in the blue shade of the mango trees, were waiting for me; others smoked short pipes, their babies slung on their backs. The midwife, tattooed, toothless, dried up—a great fetisher—came to meet me.

"*Eso bedo*, Doéllé," she said, adjusting a cloth adorned with printed bicycles and locomotives.

"*Eso bedo*, Akadu."

Thank you for yesterday. Yes. But what has tomorrow in store?

2

*Nyo nu e nyi esi fafa ke nou na ame
enyi esi wo gû ke me wo ku na eto kule.*

(Woman is a cold pool that kills, a deep
pool that drowns.)

WE WERE in the little dispensary. Between two
stacks of dressings, mosquito larvae were squirming in
a jar.

"These are stegomyias, carriers of yellow fever,"
Capitaine Docteur was saying. "I wonder when the Ad-
ministration will make up its mind to drain the lagoons,
or at least pour enough oil over them. When you visit
the huts, Doéllé, see that the women never leave water
standing in their jars. Give orders in every village for
all garbage to be burned and all pits filled in: it's the only
way to—"

24

At that instant a shriek of fear came from the doctor's bungalow. I saw Capitaine Docteur turn pale, but with clenched jaws he strove to maintain his calm before the African assistants, who were watching him. He set down the jar of stegomyias on the table. Fresh cries broke out, and now without more ado he thrust past me and made for his house, whither I followed him at a run.

"The Parisienne is frightened of everything," I thought. "I suppose she's found a rat under the bed."

And then I saw her! She was stumbling about, naked save for a blue satin wrapper, with her hair in disorder. A great python encircled her ankle and was climbing up her legs. She had been raising a *seko* when she saw this snake slipping along the veranda. No doubt it was more frightened than she was; but she didn't know that it was a god out for a stroll from the neighboring temple, and calling to the boys for help, she struck it on the head, twice. Being used to the veneration of the faithful and to every token of the humblest respect, it flew into a rage.

Urgèle, feeling herself progressively bound, struggled in vain to free herself from the living noose. She was very pale and looked like one of the martyrs in the pictures at the Mission; but she was shrieking uncontrollably and her torn garment revealed her breasts.

With all his strength Capitaine Docteur sought to force the python to release its hold, but it spat furiously, its tongue flashing in and out and its jaws emitting the vile stench common to creatures of slow digestion. It began to tighten its coils around Urgèle, so that already she felt a chill, relentless pressure at her waist.

"Stop screaming!" ordered the doctor, panting from his efforts. "And don't be afraid: pythons aren't venomous."

The petrified boys were looking less at the snake than at the white woman's breasts. Capitaine Docteur hurled appalling curses at them and they leaped back. Then he snatched up a hunting knife that lay on the desk—one that he used as a paper-cutter—and plunged it into the python's right eye, cutting, stabbing, and turning the blade deep in the wound. Blood spurted onto Urgèle's bosom and face and covered the doctor's white overall, while the python's tail began violently thrashing the floor as if the knife, far from causing death, had given it fresh strength.

Urgèle's eyes dilated. She was living in a nightmare and saw herself being suffocated before the eyes of her husband, the nurse, and the boys, yet beyond their help. But slowly the muscular coils relaxed their hold, paused for a second, and then dropped to the floor.

Blood was trickling over the mat as Madame Docteur surveyed the python writhing in agony at her feet. This time it was the Blessed Virgin that I thought of: she was dressed in blue too, and in the church she crushed a serpent beneath her sovereign heel.

Then Urgèle collapsed and Capitaine Docteur caught her, limp and colorless, in his arms.

"Don't stand there gaping!" he said to me roughly. "Make haste and give her an injection of camphorated oil, and tell Kanjo to scrub the floor and bury the python."

The boys, who had prudently withdrawn, crept back on the tips of their bare toes. At the sight of the snake twisting in its death throes Bokari and Kankwe groaned, while the Child of the Moon fled weeping behind the coconut palms. Yaya, bowing to the python, pressed his hands to his eyes, while I, in the sudden grip of ancestral beliefs, was afraid, afraid. . . .

"Why all this fuss?" asked Urgèle weakly, raising herself on the bed that she had stained with blood. "Everything's all right now that you've killed it, Frantz."

"It was a very special snake," answered the doctor as with a worried air he soaked a sponge in a basin of hot water. "To the natives it's a god. Not long ago they'd have burned anyone alive who killed it."

"We called it Grandfather," I put in curtly, handing Urgèle a glass of gin, "and we look upon it as an emanation of the rainbow."

I was outraged, though only dimly understanding the fury that shook me. Old, forgotten pictures sprang sharply to my mind. In my mother's hut mutton was never eaten; the story ran that once, long ago, Dangbé the python escaped from a great fire, thanks to a sheep that allowed him to roll himself around its fleece; therefore Dangbé's adepts had sworn never again to eat sheep's flesh.

"The python god should have lived. What signifies the death of a white woman?" protested my secret heart,

27

while Capitaine Docteur as he put on another starched white overall said to Urgèle, "When you get up you'll see beyond the lagoon a few mud huts. That's the Snake Temple, ruled by the great fetish priestess Deno, Mother of Prayers. As the gods may not be locked up, pythons wander freely about Manoho. Any native would be proud to find one curled up on his mat, and think it an honor to miss eggs from his poultry yard. Of course you couldn't guess that this spectacular visitor was a god come to greet you. Pythons are harmless as a rule and I can't make out why this one went for you. I suppose your screaming and hitting it with the *seko* stick maddened it. This is a very nasty business; the fetishers are sure to make trouble for me."

The boys had retired into the dim kitchen, but I could still hear Bokari's groans. To have seen a dead python was a terrific experience for them. They had sealed its grave with a small stone which they would later take to the Mother of Prayers together with the required offerings: palm oil, yams, guinea fowls, and tricolor cloth. But they must also make purification by bathing; they must rub their foreheads with a sacred powder to ward off the vengeance of Dangbé the python, and shave their heads. Without these precautions it was certain that Dangbé would cause them all to die of dropsy.

And I said to myself, "No purifying bath can cleanse the python's blood from the breasts of the two white people. No sacrifice will avert disaster from this house. In the old days when an evildoer denied his crimes they subjected him to the Dangbé test. A python if hung about the neck of an innocent man would withdraw without harming him; but if it wanted to prove his guilt it would fly into a rage and seek to strangle him. For Dangbé to have given such violent proof of his displeasure Urgèle must be black with invisible sins!"

She was still pale and tense as I turned to her and said in my most honeyed tones, "The boys are worried because the killing of a python is a very bad omen. But don't think any more about it, Madame Docteur. Another time if you come upon a snake like that, call the fetisher; he'll come and collect it in a white cloth and take it back to the temple with the veneration due to a god."

At that moment someone clapped his hands at the foot of the steps and a white man, the agricultural officer, presented himself. Looking absurd, as he usually did, with his tight mouth of a miser, he bowed to Urgèle.

He was followed by boys carrying palm branches, plumed euonymus, the decorative leaves of the breadfruit, and the green and yellow motley of croton. I remembered then that it was Christmas. Other boys were coming upstairs similarly laden; they laid flamboyants on the table, and scented, waxy frangipanis. There were also purslane flowers, and fruit so lovely that one could hardly bring oneself to eat it: custard apples of exquisite corruption. Last of all came a child delicately holding three roses in his pale palms. Three roses, touching in their fragility, valiantly blooming beneath the pitiless sun; three roses without thorn or scent.

A benevolent fetish had suddenly caused a whole garden to blossom on that sullied veranda.

"We will efface the python's hateful blood!" cried the scents and colors. "Forget, forget! We've come to bring you hope—we are joy!"

And Urgèle, the white witch, heard the reviving clamor as clearly as I. I saw her leap up; with eyes closed she plunged her hands among the sprays, breathed the vital sap of the leaves, inhaled the chaos of scents.

"I love it," she was saying. "I love it all. . . ."

As a modest craftsman withdraws before his work, so the agricultural officer stood humbly in the background.

That evening the doctor was giving a dinner for his wife, and the Christmas tree had to be decorated. At the Sisters' I was always given this task. "You're an artist in your way, Doéllé," Mother Saint-Ange would say, "but beware of pride. Your gift is from God."

A *filao* tree had been put in the corner of the dining room and I set to work hanging gold and silver threads among its delicate foliage. Serene once more, Madame Docteur handed me paper stars, colored angels, and shining comets. Bokari and the Child of the Moon brought me the stepladder; they clucked for joy as if they had never in their lives beheld a dead python. In the twinkling of an eye the flowers and greenery had banished the avenging spirits from the house—but they are not so easily defeated. Sometimes they pretend to

30

yield, only to rush in again when one has forgotten all about them.

At the end of the veranda Amalia continued to hem dusters with an air of distaste. From time to time she would lean her elbows on the sill beneath the raised *seko* to stare at the lagoon; her profile had a stillness that seemed of eternity. She had not so much as turned her head at the slaying of the python; Urgèle's screams moved her no more than the bringing of the enchanted Christmas boughs. She went on sewing, indifferent to it all. Sometimes I heard her sigh.

"I don't know anyone at the post yet," said Madame Docteur. "Please, Doéllé, tell me how many are coming and who they are."

"Well, there'll be the agricultural officer whom you've just seen, Madame Docteur. His job is to count cassava plants and reckon the areas planted with yams, check graters and nut-shelling machines, select trees and test fertilizers and new implements. He doesn't seem to find any of this very interesting. I hardly know what does interest him, except money. The cry of the flying foxes keeps him awake, so he plugs up his ears with bread pellets, but he's careful to save all the crusts in a tin and takes them with him to Bordeaux every time he goes home, for his mother's dog. 'There are *no* minor economies,' he says."

Like the boys, Madame Docteur seemed to have forgotten the morning's terrors, and she laughed as she unfolded the pink tablecloth embroidered by the Sisters.

31

"And who are the other guests?"

"There's the cassava planter—everyone calls him *le père* Lambert. He's seventy and has been in the colonies for fifty years. He was scene-shifter at the Châtelet theater in Paris, and once when they put on 'Around the World in Eighty Days' the stage sets made him long to see real coconut palms and live panthers. From Dei Tham to the New Hebrides, via Pointe-Noire, his life has been one long adventure—and his stories of it make decent people blush. But when once he starts there's no hope of turning a deaf ear: he shouts, you see. Whether he's at the cassava market or a reception at Government House, old Lambert always shouts. At night when he wakes up and feels bored he shouts again, for fun; and his parrot—he's got a parrot with a vocabulary about as respectable as his own—the parrot screeches in imitation."

"And does his wife shriek too?"

"Oh no! She was once a Sister of Charity. She was nursing lepers in Dahomey when he carried her off. Sometimes she's overcome with remorse to think how she broke her word to God, and then to hide her distress she laughs. You'll often hear them from your house, Madame Docteur. Old Lambert bellows at imaginary enemies, the ex-nun shouts with laughter, and the parrot, frantic with the noise, mimics them each in turn."

"And I'm so fond of silence, Doéllé. . . . Tell me about the District Officer. Is he as excitable as the cassava man?"

"He's no longer young and there's a bitter look on his

face. He misses the big hunting expeditions in Ubangi, in the days when a D.O. was a sort of king among the natives. He spends most of his time at the Residency offices and occupies his mind by writing ethnographical works. He doesn't have much fun at home. His wife, as a result of blackwater fever, suffers from depression; she just sits there looking tired and knitting useless things."

"Then in Manoho there's not a single white woman who's young and attractive?" asked Madame Docteur uneasily. I repressed a smile. She was wondering whom her husband could have been paying court to while he was alone here.

"Yes, there's the wife of Marit the schoolmaster, Madame Elisabeth. She slanders the women and tries to seduce the men. She's quite pretty, but her wrists and ankles are bleached in a queer way—they're covered with white patches. She thinks a lot about love and talks of nothing else, so certain people here like her. Even the D.O. is said to—"

"You know everything, Doéllé!" said Madame Docteur, smiling, as she placed knife-rests, shaped like lizards, on the tablecloth.

"Pretty much everything, Madame Docteur. Every detail in this place is noticed and passed on from boy to boy and house to house. No truck can leave Manoho without the natives knowing at what time it left and where it went, and how and why."

"So I'm to expect seven guests this evening. You haven't forgotten anyone, Doéllé?"

33

"Apart from the schoolmaster, Marit, who's completely Africanized and can no longer bear the idea of returning to France, I've described all the inhabitants of Manoho, Madame Docteur. There's no one else."

Why did I lie? Why did I deny that another guest was expected that evening: Flavien the magistrate, my lover? Did I foolishly hope to avert danger by not pronouncing his name, and by hiding from Urgèle how unstable he was, how cruel—and how attractive? Yet I knew that to fight one must see clearly. Does not the Ewe proverb say: "To gather the fruit of the palm one must first thrust aside the branches"?

Meanwhile, as always when in the grip of some anxiety, I felt damp all over. A bitterness in my mouth and my repeated yawns gave warning of a bout of malaria. We Africans are exposed from infancy to the bites of mosquitoes, which make whining, skinny, thirsty babies of us—that is, if we live. If we survive the third year we have acquired immunity, and as adults we're hardly ever troubled by malaria. Yet like the white people I was subject to these repeated and most depressing attacks. It was true that for the last three months I had unwisely omitted my daily dose of quinine; for although the doctor constantly declared that this drug did not induce miscarriage, I was afraid it might make me sterile. And I so longed to bear Flavien an almost white child.

I was shivering with fever when at eight that evening I saw Madame Docteur coming from the shower. Sweat already beaded her freshly powdered face. Her fair hair was dressed in braids about her head like a halo, and she wore a clinging black dress, strangely gathered, and falling in folds to the ankles. The frock seemed to me very simple and unadorned, yet outrageous in its smartness. I had never seen a white woman dressed like that in Manoho. A whiff of scent floated about her.

Capitaine Docteur had asked me to see to the *réveillon*, the midnight supper: dressed crab, chicken with ground nuts, fillet of beef, and pineapple tart. From my place behind the icebox I could watch the arrival of the guests. They had the formal, starched air they feel constrained to assume on festive occasions. The boys began laughing and called them "scraped pigs," *mâchoirons*— a certain fish in the lagoon which is all jaw—and *pique-boeufs*, dressed in white as pure as that of the birds so named: the egrets that live on the backs of sheep and remove their parasites.

Loud of voice and with his shock of white hair even more on end than usual, old Lambert arrived first, followed by the ex-nun, whose flowered cretonne frock made her look fat and lumpy. The schoolmaster was already drunk when he came up the steps, and Madame Elisabeth as she greeted Urgèle had as malignant an air as the python of the morning. I was almost surprised not to see a black forked tongue dart from her reddened lips. The agricultural officer was ill at ease in his evening clothes, and wiped his moist hands unceasingly with his handkerchief. Then came the D.O., haughty and preoccupied; but at the sight of Urgèle fifteen years slipped from his shoulders. His wife followed him like a shadow,

35

carrying a little basketwork bag that contained beige-colored knitting.

They were all drinking brandy and water when the one I was waiting for appeared: Flavien!

He bent his cropped head before Urgèle in apparent diffidence.

"Forgive me, Madame," he said, with the air of gravity that never left him. "A dead child was found under a banyan near Tabligno, and I had to go there. Please excuse my lateness."

Madame Docteur seemed surprised by this unexpected guest, whose name had not been given her. She ordered a place to be laid for him at the end of the table, and the dinner began. It was a dinner I shall never forget.

No one spoke. The men, transfixed, stared in stupefaction at Urgèle—at her blonde halo and the black frock that clung to her like a second skin. From the outset the atmosphere was intolerably oppressive. Everyone looked at her: the D.O., the schoolmaster, the old cassava planter, even the harmless agriculturalist. Flavien as much as the rest, and more.

White witch! By her mere presence she held them spellbound, speechless; she drew their gaze like a magnet. And I, hidden behind a curtain, could do nothing to break that spell. The other women were as powerless as myself to avert the danger. The ex-nun didn't feel like laughing that evening. Madame Commandant, the D.O.'s wife, surveyed Urgèle with a look of agony, while Madame Elisabeth shot savage glances at the doctor.

"I'm furious," she seemed to be crying, as her foot tapped nervously beneath the table. "You're impossible, marrying such a strange female. Why couldn't you bring an ordinary wife to Manoho?"

That dinner! A sticky wind from the sea billowed the cotton hangings on the wall, and the inexorable boom of surf along the bar filled the room. "Talk, talk! Break this frightful silence!" I cried inwardly; and as if she heard me, Madame Docteur began to ask random questions about the country, hunting, and python temples. She received only brief and scrappy answers. These men, united but yesterday in a vague alliance, felt themselves slipping back into primitive savagery. Each of them wanted her for himself, and soon. Who would win? The air about Urgèle became as dense as with us during the great "drums," when the fetisher falls unconscious, foaming at the mouth.

Bokari changed the plates for the beef, and at that moment Madame Docteur clumsily dropped her fork. Before Bokari could fetch another, five silver forks were held out to her with excessive eagerness. "Please take mine!" begged the five looks of the D.O., cassava planter, schoolmaster, agricultural officer, and Flavien. "Take *my* fork, not one of the others!"

They all waited for her to make her choice; a choice which they foolishly invested with the value of a symbol. She hesitated, smiled—and I must acknowledge that her teeth were as dazzling as my own—and then extended her hand toward the doctor, who was drumming on the table with feigned indifference.

"I'll take my husband's fork," she said, "as he's the only man who didn't offer it."

The sticky wind continued to blow through the *sekos* and the sickly scent of the custard apples grew heavier. Flavien had pushed away his plate and was glaring at Urgèle in amazement and anger. He gazed at her fixedly as if to transmit a secret command. Madame Docteur was being smothered by these imprisoning stares.

At last to everyone's relief the planter broke the spell. He had drunk a great deal and his florid cheeks were now the color of garnets. He addressed Urgèle in his coarse voice.

"Well, Madame, what do you think of Manoho? I expect you were told a lot of tales about Africa when you were in Paris, eh? I can imagine the sort of thing. All the people who've never so much as set foot in Dakar and abuse the country for the fun of it. The colonial has an easy life, they'll tell you, with a Negress in his lap and a bottle of whisky in his hand. And the rubbish they'll have tried to make you swallow! Have you heard of the boy who chews up the meat balls before serving them? Or the one who lets the oil fall drop by drop from his mouth to make the mayonnaise? And the women's robes that they soak in milk to turn it into cheese? Eh? Have you heard of them?"

"No," said Urgèle coldly. "I've been told mostly of mosquitoes and sunstroke."

"Don't you believe it, Madame!" cried the planter with warmth. "Mosquitoes and sunstroke don't exist. By rights I should be dead twenty times over. *Trompe-la-Mort*—Cheat-Death—is what they call me. My right hand? Devoured by a cannibal at Port-Villa. My left? Gangrened to the bone in Gabon. I've had blackwater fever in Senegal, yellow fever on the Gold Coast, and sleeping sickness in Dahomey. And sound as a bell, though I'm seventy. If you like I'll teach you a native language. I speak Ga as well as Ashanti, Hausa, and Mina. I learned mosquito-net grammar, as we say here. What do you think of the method, Flavien? And you, Marit? As soon as I got to know a language really well I changed the woman. There's nothing like a live dictionary."

The ex-nun began fidgeting on her chair and gave little nervous coughs. The agricultural officer thought a diversion might be welcome; he wiped his moist fingers on a pink table napkin and bravely addressed Urgèle.

"I'm sure, Madame, that you would prefer the climate and customs of Tahiti. Before my appointment here I worked for three years at Paéa; it was delightful. There were lagoons there of crystal-clear water, full of blue coral and fish like rubies. And those sunsets, Madame, for one with a soul for such things! Those sunsets, purple over Moorea! In Tahiti, you see—"

For the agricultural officer Tahiti was an obsession, an eternal regret, an ideal. Whenever he met a European he could never refrain from sprinkling his conversation with the words guitar, tiaré, vahiné, paréo, regardless of context. But his voice was so flat and neutral as to dim even the brightest images, and no one ever paid attention to what he said. That evening again he talked into a void, his monologue a tepid stream that flowed on unhindered by the others. Flavien continued to gaze sternly and silently at Urgèle; his right eye, narrowed in concentration, gave him an expression of brutal intensity. I had seen that look only once before, when he was angry with a native and had given him three lashes of the *chicote* across the shoulders. I wondered whether he admired Madame Docteur or loathed her—whether he wanted to take her in his arms or beat her. I've learned since that this is what they call passion.

The chill was off the champagne, the set piece was collapsing and the kirsch ice was melting in sluggish trickles. Urgèle shook her little haloed head to free herself from silence and the slow stares; she jingled her bracelets as if to snap invisible chains. As Yaya served the champagne she turned toward her neighbor, the District Officer.

"I'm very ignorant," she said with a little smile. "Would you tell me one day just what your work consists of?"

She knew that a man is always at ease when talking of his profession; and indeed the D.O. now relaxed, gratified at last by her interest in him.

"At the moment," he told her, "I'm just a bureaucrat poring over ledgers, reports, and statistics. For the sake of abstract ideas—that are still of only problematical value—all that gave the administrator his power and efficiency has been destroyed. In the old days the work was absorbing. We weren't gagged then by political considerations: the natives recognized one master, their D.O.—their father and their mother, sole dispenser of punishments, sole judge of criminal offenses. Our powers and prestige are greatly at a discount with them now. Gone are the days when the D.O. could make free use of credits and local labor, so that he could, without great expense, build schools and dispensaries, dig wells in the bush and build roads. What I liked above all, Madame, were the roads. The riding away before dawn, the staking out . . ."

"And meanwhile," interrupted the resigned voice of his wife, "I was left alone at home. I had neither chairs nor saucepans, and a panther killed and ate my dog and the guinea fowl I'd tamed."

The D.O. waved away this intrusion into his discourse and went on. "I nursed those roads as if they'd been my children, through rock and mud. I planted kapok and teak which had to be lovingly guarded against browsing animals and devouring fire. But years afterward, when one travels that road again in a car— believe me, Madame, it's really moving to see the woods that have taken the place of those tender saplings; the fruits that have followed the buds. It almost seems that even in this futile world one may have left one's name to a useful piece of work."

"You're very lyrical, *monsieur l'administrateur!*" said

41

the schoolmaster mockingly, throwing out his short arms above the flamboyants on the table. "But where are all your wooden bridges now—your mud dispensaries and your famous roads? They were only temporary. Oh, I'm not denying your skill, and at the time you had very limited means. But it all has to be done again with sheet iron and cement, with bulldozers that crush cubic meters of ground at a time, and buffalo pumps that squirt insecticides to giddy heights. You talk in the past tense, as if the D.O.'s job was at an end. Not a bit of it! But machines have changed the face of Africa and we must begin again on a fresh basis. The pioneering work is done, but the administrator's is only beginning. It's he who'll be the link between the Colonial Empire and the French Union."

The schoolmaster's tone, ironic at first, had risen in anger. He grew flushed and gesticulated ever more vehemently, while the D.O.'s face hardened.

"What do you expect?" he replied. "I'm of the old school, but it seems to me that in my day when there were no machines things were no worse than they are now. Ask any African, Marit. If he's sufficiently Europeanized and if he trusts you, he'll probably tell you that his present rôle of guinea pig is becoming more onerous and difficult every day."

"In Tahiti, now, we never had these problems," ventured the agricultural officer, who felt a fresh storm rising and sought to avert it. "I remember a case in the Leeward Islands—"

But once more his colorless murmur proved ineffectual, and it was Capitaine Docteur who, speaking for the first time, addressed the schoolmaster.

"Marit, you seem a bit nervy these days. You'd better come and see me one morning—although I believe the only medicine you need is French mountain air. I think you'll get your leave soon."

From red the schoolmaster's face turned to crimson; he gulped a glass of iced champagne.

"Leave?" he stammered. "Don't talk to me of leave. I'm sick at the mere idea of sailing. You make plans— new dresses for madame, the Place de la Concorde flood-lit, and the Champs Élysées. Then you go ashore. It's cold. You're ashamed of your clothes. You've forgotten how to choose things in the shops and what tip to give the taxi driver. Life's too expensive. All your friends are away and relations treat you as if you were country cousins—and not quite right in the head at that. You feel poor. In France we colonials are beyond the pale."

"And that's why last time you made us take the first boat back to Africa!" cried Madame Elisabeth acidly. "And *la petite* was in such need of French air."

La petite was there at a separate table; now and then she turned very feminine eyes toward the grownups with somewhat embarrassing coquetry. Madame Elisa-beth having heard sinister tales of rape never dared en-trust her daughter to the care of the boys, but took her with her everywhere to cocktail parties and dinners, where everyone felt obliged to pinch the child's cheek, admire her short embroidered frocks and ask, "How are you, Adeline? You look very well. Are you enjoying

43

yourself? What's that lovely doll called? Have you been good? That's splendid—keep it up!" And the little girl, who perpetually carried a celluloid doll slung on her back, in imitation of the native mothers carrying their babies, behaved like a kitten being fondled, and was in fact bored to death.

The conversation turned for a time to children. The ex-nun, at ease at last as on a calm sea unthreatened by squalls, began talking volubly. But she irritated me. They all did: old Lambert, the D.O., and the schoolmaster, with their colonial habit of letting the most trivial conversation degenerate into a quarrel. After all, they were playing quite secondary parts; they remained in shadow. The real drama was between the silent—terribly silent—hero and heroine, Flavien and Urgèle, who spoke not a word but gazed the more intently at and into one another. Indeed they were somehow alike; they were already united by I know not what strange bonds. Separated by the width of the table they were yet twin branches from the same stem, two feline creatures of the same species. Do we not belong, like animals and plants, to certain families? Urgèle and Flavien recognized one another though they had never met before. And a proverb came into my mind: "When the snail travels he lodges with the tortoise." Or as white people say: "Birds of a feather flock together."

I knew myself powerless in the face of destiny, and all at once I felt so weary and limp with fever that I left my hiding place. The boys didn't hear me coming in my leather sandals; they were drinking red wine from bottles stolen from the store.

"Well, Yaya? Kankwe? And you Bokari?" I exclaimed severely. But Madame Docteur appeared at the end of the veranda, very straight in the black dress that fell in folds to her ankle; Madame Docteur came toward me, dabbing her moist forehead.

"Thank you, Doéllé, for having supervised the dinner so well. It was perfect. The boys may clear the table now; we're going to dance. But what's the matter with you? You're feverish—you're ill, Doéllé! Quickly, fetch all you want from the kitchen for your sister Océa and then get to bed."

They were going to dance; and I was being sent away. I was used to it. All the same it hurt. . . .

At the maternity clinic the light was on in the hut where two women were seriously ill. They lay quite motionless, waiting for death perhaps, their clothes pulled up over their breasts. I lay down near them on a camp bed. Would Flavien dance with Urgèle?

Suddenly I heard the squealing of the gramophone in a vague tune, losing itself in the noise of the breakers on the beach. An old tune that I had heard on the boat coming back from Dakar. White people had danced to it at the end of the promenade deck; it was a gala evening on board and I had listened to the music from a distance, as I was listening now. I remembered that they had thrown streamers at one another, joylessly, and the stewards had gathered up these faded ribbons and pitched them overboard like any other seaweed—like dead snakes.

A voice from the bungalow dragged me from these memories and made me start; it drowned the dull roar of the waves and the whining of the gramophone. "I want a drink!" old Lambert was shouting.

3

Dsèn onmoo nè.

(One must adorn oneself to please.)

NEXT morning before the Christmas Mass I called at the Mission to greet the Sisters. Their pale faces, looking smaller for the coifs and sun helmets above them, were radiant.

"There, Doéllé!" cried Mother Saint-Ange. "Divine grace will always reach the sinner in the end. Old Lambert who has never entered a church in his life, who dared to elope with a servant of God and who insults the divine mercy every moment of the day—old Lambert has repented. Come and see."

She took me masterfully by the hand as if I had been still the little nine-year-old child snatched from fetish

47

cults, instead of the *évoluée* of whom she was now so proud.

"I came to Africa a long time ago," she said, much moved. "A sailor took charge of my poor little luggage on the boat and was so attentive to me when I landed that I gave him all my wealth: a five-franc note. That sailor, as you'll have guessed, was Monsieur Lambert, who has since grown so great. And do you know what he's sent to the Mission this morning? A magnificent refrigerator! 'To Mother Saint-Ange, in memory of a five-franc note.' That's what he's written on his visiting card, under his name."

A refrigerator! For people who live in the tropics the inventor of radio is no doubt a genius, but what are we to say of the one who devised the refrigerator? I beheld the Sisters clustered about this unhoped-for treasure as about the Blessed Sacrament itself. They clasped their hands in ecstasy. And the little African girls, their ewe lambs, in frocks too short for them and with their breasts tightly compressed, cackled their enthusiasm.

Mother Saint-Ange rummaged busily in a mildewed cardboard box in search of the freshest and cleanest holy pictures, that she might send them immediately with her thanks to the sentimental tapioca merchant. The animation of these bleached women filled me for a moment with regret for the days when I learned arithmetic, grammar, and singing among them; I didn't know then whether they meant to make a typist of me, or a dressmaker, a schoolmistress, or a nurse, but they assured me that at the end of the road I should find peace of heart

48

and the anchor of certainty. And in those far distant days I was happy because I believed blindly in their promises.

The bells began to ring and I followed the Sisters to the church, falling behind as they moved up into the choir. One must feel very proud of one's soul to be able to come so close to God. I have always been afraid in church; I feel smothered and have to stay near the door so as to run away if anything should happen.

Kneeling near the holy water stoup I watched the natives arriving, clad in lovely, graceful blankets of many dusky, overlapping colors. Some of the cottons, printed in Manchester, had patterns of clocks, trucks, toothbrushes, and razors. One of the doctor's nursing orderlies sported a suit of shot taffeta. A recent bride had replaced her wreath of tarlatan roses on her fuzzy hair. I wore a cloth covered with red hearts through which, in token of unhappy love, were thrust open penknives. At hip level a proverb proclaimed: "*Dsèn on-moo nè!*": One must adorn oneself to please.

Through the unglazed windows I looked at swaying palm trees and thatched roofs gleaming in the sun, while the interpreter repeated the priest's words in Mina.

"Aren't you ashamed? What would *le bon Dieu* think of me if I behaved like you and lay down to celebrate Mass?"

The priest had interrupted the reading of the Epistle to blast with voice and gaze the Mina children prone along the benches, and the women whose heads were

49

already nodding. At that moment the white people entered the church.

Foreigners indeed! We hardly recognized them. To celebrate Christmas worthily they had seen fit to dress themselves like people in France. On getting up that morning they had said to themselves: "Let's find out whether that dark suit is still fit to be seen or whether the termites have had it all." They had opened tin trunks, redolent of naphthaline, to take out and shake trousers that had lost their creases, and crumpled waistcoats, and they now appeared in navy-blue suits that cramped their shoulders and made their skin look paler than ever. Madame Commandant was wearing silk stockings on which sweat appeared in uneven patches. Madame Elisabeth had exchanged her sun helmet for a quaint hat adorned with artificial flowers and surrounded by one of those tiny mosquito nets they call veils.

With even more dignity than usual they climbed to the narrow gallery above the choir; it is reserved for them every Sunday so that the smell of our black skins may not offend their nostrils.

"Why is Madame Docteur not with them?" I wondered. "Has last night's dancing so tired her that she prefers to rest at home?"

With us, curiosity is easily aroused, but is fitful, and dies as quickly as it is born. A second later I thought no more of Urgèle's absence but was studying the crèche, surrounded by cardboard rocks, that the pupils of the Fathers had made: St. Joseph was in shorts and the

Virgin wore a European dress with a pith helmet. Gone were the days when our craftsmen, looked upon as magicians, derived their most striking effects from animist inspiration. Then they were loaded with favors, they followed our kings and chiefs and portrayed their feats on panels of bronze. . . .

"Life in Africa moves too quickly now," I thought. "Kings can no longer maintain artists who may spend years on a single work, and chiefs prefer photographs to carvings. Where the ancestor cult is waning artists cease to represent it, and they now take the style of Saint-Sulpice for their model. But catholicism has not sunk its roots deep enough into our hearts for any spring of inspiration to well from them. And Negro art, as the whites say, is dying. . . ."

A slight sound aroused me from these melancholy thoughts. Flavien was leading Madame Docteur to one of the back benches.

Flavien at church! It was extraordinary. He never went to Mass, even on Armistice Day. I was just behind them, but the magistrate, absorbed in his sudden devotion, had not noticed me. The priest was beginning to read the gospel, but instead of listening to it with proper reverence, Flavien was looking at Urgèle. Later when the worshipers rose he touched her bare arm—her wrist. Her profile was rigid beneath her helmet as she feigned unconsciousness. She seemed absent in body and soul. But I shook with rage to see Flavien bending over her missal, shoulder against shoulder.

"What sin!" I said to myself, seeing him behave thus in church. "But how is it he's with Urgèle, away from the others? I can guess—once desire drives him, nothing can hold him back; he keeps his eyes on his goal and flattens all obstacles before him. He must have planned carefully to get Madame Docteur alone like this: he must have called as if by chance at the hospital and offered her a lift in his station wagon, which is more comfortable than the medical truck, and then staged a breakdown to delay them. Flavien's ingenuity knows no bounds where his passions are involved."

For communion the women drew their blankets up to the shoulder and the Sisters' pupils in their short pink frocks moved toward the altar with bowed heads. At this holy moment Flavien, instead of inclining his head, turned deliberately to Urgèle and said almost aloud, "Isn't all this color amazing? Of course black skin sets off almost anything. But wait till you visit Guinea—Youkoukoun, for instance. There you'll see men at communion wearing nothing but a tiny basket instead of a loincloth."

He touched Madame Docteur, he looked at her, he talked to her during Mass! Indignation choked me. What natives say of white people's shamelessness is no slander. I resolved to call on Flavien at siesta time and make him see reason. Others had been watching his disgraceful behavior, and if he meant to keep his prestige as magistrate he would have to reform his ways.

Meanwhile the Christmas Mass came to an end. With full-dress smiles the Europeans went to their cars; the sticky heat had rendered their Parisian clothes unbearable. But at the sound of joyful cries my face relaxed: my sister Océa was waiting for me near the Mission, demonstrative and impetuous as ever in her affection. She was even more beautiful than usual. Her bare breasts gleamed with cosmetics and down around her hips was draped an *avotata* of downy velvet striped with pink and black. She used clove scent and had drawn a line of antimony along her eyelids, while a little powdered chalk absorbed the sweat on her neck.

"How lovely to see you, Océa!"

"You never come to Waji now, so I got a lift into Manoho to talk to you. Mother's angry; she says you forget the respect due to old people and widows, and that you never come home now because you're too fond of white people."

"Mother forgets how much work a nurse has to do; there's not time to go as far as Waji. But I'll come soon. Now I'm free until two o'clock, so let's go to the store. I want to buy you some canned goods and some presents. What a pretty *duku* you've wound round your head!"

She walked beside me gaily, carrying her raised hands like precious things, palms upward to the sun.

No other girl had the grace of my sister Océa. She had been to school with the boys for a short time, but she learned parrot fashion without attempting to understand. Her attention was easily distracted and she quickly lost interest. The African schoolmaster had done

53

little to stimulate her intellect, as to him the education of girls from the bush seemed unnecessary. My
mother had been glad to have Océa back in the hut with
her, saying that her youngest daughter at least should
be preserved from European contacts and continue to
live according to the laws of our fathers.

At the store, which was kept by two friends, Optimist
and Philanthropist, one could buy hurricane lamps,
blankets, white cotton thread, toys, sulphur, quinine,
and bicycles. I bought tinned peaches and some English
jam for Océa, and was putting out my hand to a pot of
honey when she gave a little cry.

"No, no, Doéllé—not honey! Fossou's not allowed
to eat it."

"Fossou?"

"My sweetheart," she said, lowering her long lashes.
"He lives at Agokpamé. He serves the fetish Agbami
whose symbol is the bee, and so the eating of honey is
forbidden to him. I'm going to marry him soon. In another month he'll send mother some bottles of liqueur,
and money—and he's promised to put three fine gold
ornaments in my *batsisi*."

Mother would be glad. Her elder daughter was losing
her soul by living like a European, but at least the
younger would remain faithful to tradition and forge
new, sound links in the chain. Who knows? Mother
may have been right. If the greater number of Africa's
children today listen to the white man's teachings, it is
well that some should turn resolutely away from progress and cleave to the old gods. In fifty years' time the

European will be able to judge. Will he then find the true *évolués* among the natives in soft hats who have become lawyers and doctors, or among those like Océa and Fossou who will be following their own path of spiritual progress? A white man would laugh to hear me say this; yet no one knows what may become of us in the future. . . .

This is what I was thinking as I opened a tin of peaches for Océa at the hospital. She was hopping round me like a bird, carefree and happy. She had not lost the serenity of her race, nor had civilization taught her to puzzle herself with vain questions.

"How pretty your new neighbor is—Madame Docteur!" she said suddenly. "Has she given you lots of presents? I saw her just now; she had on a violet dress and was going into Fio Kanate's hut with Capitaine Docteur. They say he's had some *calalu* made for them and for two African doctors. Tell me, is she really pretty, or is it just that she seems so? But you're bleeding, Doéllé! You've cut yourself!"

At the mere mention of Urgèle my lurking anger flared up, the can opener slipped under my hand, and my blood was now dripping heavily to the floor. "Let her stay with King Fio Kanate," I was thinking. "I shall visit *my* king: Flavien whom I love." And having abruptly dismissed my astonished sister I set off for the courthouse.

The sun poured vertically onto the lagoon, and the red earth was scorching. I pictured Madame Docteur drinking tepid champagne before a row of empty armchairs representing five generations of ancestors. Pigs and dwarf goats wandered freely about the seat of majesty on which sat Fio Kanate V. I had often seen him. He dressed in the style of Louis XV; in the red, gold and embroideries of a glittering theatrical costume, strayed, heaven knows how, to Manoho. On the wall hung a photograph in which he wore a white bonnet with frills. I could already hear Madame Docteur's description of the meal. Dignitaries, their blankets dropped to the waist in token of deference, made ready to serve pink pawpaws and insipid avocado pears in palm oil; then the *calalu*—half smoked fish, half meat and chicken —accompanied by yam and cassava paste drowned in fiery *pili-pili* sauce. The guests would certainly be offered *boma,* a dish of Portuguese origin, and a bowl of tapioca seasoned with cinnamon. Then girls would come in and sing the interminable history of the *Ghens'* migrations from the Gold Coast. I pictured Urgèle: half-dazzled with light, she would behold with disgust through the open window the king's wives relieving themselves on the beach, and black pigs rooting among the garbage. "So this is lunch with a Negro king," she would reflect, as she turned her face to the fleeting coolness of the punkah. Such kings at their death had slaves sacrificed to escort them to the realm of shades, where they continued to serve them.

Still thinking of Madame Docteur I crossed the cemetery, which, starting at the sea, thrusts the last of its graves untidily behind the courthouse. Here and there among the palm-fanned mounds rose a hastily fashioned, sand-scoured cross with a name scrawled on it in chalk beneath the scarlet hibiscus. Broken bricks revealed a name, a date: Klara de Souza, 1884. Blazing frangipani blossoms sprawled across a broken plaque on which was inscribed: "Who sows the wind shall reap the whirlwind," or "Love him who loves you." These maxims had no connection with the skeletons moldering beneath them. Natives cared nothing for the sense; it was the music they listened to in copying down such words as pleased them. I paused for a moment before the rose-colored tomb of my uncle, Gamélé. It is in the Portuguese style, surrounded by columns of pistachio-green. The stucco is surmounted by a cross, for Gamélé was more or less Catholic; but for safety's sake my aunt had added a barbaric colored statue representing death, to which she brought a weekly offering of rice and palm wine.

I had come now to the old German cemetery. The noise of the bar did not penetrate so far; here was the final silence of solitude. Overturned stones and cracked marble received impassively the impact of fallen coconuts—the coconuts that smashed upon forgotten names: Polizeimeister Wanker, 1902. Died of yellow fever. Rosina Kenzler. Died of yellow fever. *Schlafe im Frieden. Auf Wiedersehen!*

Each time I came here I pondered the destinies of these peoples—Brazilians, Danes, Germans, English, and Frenchmen—who one after the other came to the slave coast to die there, leaving so slight a trace in the

57

snake-haunted sand. I've been taught that they were all different from one another, with temperaments and ways of living peculiar to their respective nations; but to me they were all alike. Sometimes I seemed to see them filing past in procession: their wraiths were ageless and without race.

I had arrived at the back of the courthouse. It was a new building in so modern a style of architecture that one was surprised to see beside it the cracked decrepitude of native huts. Between these symmetrical walls Flavien sat in judgment three times a week, to try cases of theft, rape, divorce, and disputes of all kinds: interminable palavers that teach patience to the most irritable of white men.

I went straight up to his room. The mosquito net was rolled up in a bundle above the bed on which, with arms folded behind his shaven head, Flavien was sleeping.

While he had been at his previous station, Wagadugu, an exploding gasoline lamp had burned him from his right shoulder to his knee, and deep scars covered half his body. But to me he was the more moving—I longed to kiss the burns that he was so ashamed of and that sometimes made him do such cruel things. I was in no hurry to wake him. When he opened his eyes it would be but to scowl, or worse still to stare as dully as a dead fish. For hours he wouldn't speak, then he would throw himself over me with a dreadful urgency, as if to cut short a hidden pain. Was it his accident that made him so strange? Some grief or remorse? What matter! Unless one wants to add the burden of other lives to one's own it's better not to know. White people trail such mysteries behind them. Their past is always painful; the embers of memory glow on and on. . . .

But Flavien had divined my silent presence. Without opening his eyes he stretched his hands toward me.

"How good you smell, Doéllé," he said sleepily. "It isn't cinnamon today, nor cloves. It's—don't tell me—let me guess—"

"It's Madame Docteur's scent," I said sourly.

"Is it? I thought I recognized it. Come here and let me smell you."

I drew away with a shake of my head, for I was reliving the scene at Mass as he pressed his shoulder against Urgèle's and slyly touched her bare arm. Flavien, who had opened his eyes at last, looked at me without moving; he was smiling as Madame Docteur sometimes did, with that curious half-smile of closed lips that gives the face a look of incredulity, of lonely suffering, or of irony.

"What's the matter with you, Doéllé? You wouldn't be jealous by any chance? Thank God there's no such thing as jealousy in your country. A man's wives understand one another perfectly, and he's free to play about away from home. No one worries him with scenes."

"You *will* not understand, Flavien! If our men keep several wives it's from necessity rather than choice. You know perfectly well that here the wife must live chastely from the beginning of conception until her baby's weaned. That's three years she spends out of her husband's bed. Then she visits her family, and that may

59

be a long way off. When her father dies she has to stay shut up in her parents' hut for a mourning period of a hundred and fifty days. When a man's deserted so long and so often he must console himself somehow. You say the wives seem to put up with each other. That's because the housework, shared between them, seems easier and that when the children all grow up together they give less trouble and anxiety. But you've tried enough cases of this sort, Flavien, to know that these wives loathe one another to the point sometimes of attempted poisoning."

I paused for breath; he was still mocking me with his eyes and his bitter mouth, and I burst out again violently.

"Besides, those customs have nothing to do with me —I'm an *évoluée*. I disapprove of polygamy and my husband shall be mine alone. Isn't there a proverb that says 'A good helmet fits only one head'?"

Flavien dragged me onto the bed beside him. His thin wrists had unsuspected strength.

"You're all excited, Doéllé! Your eyes are flashing. Listen: Between Madame Docteur and you there can be no comparison. She brings a breath of Paris with her— she's stimulating—she stirs up my sluggish wits. But you —I need you. You bring me a sort of peace—you make me forget my frightful loneliness. Do you see?"

"I see," I answered peevishly, "but don't squeeze my arm like that—you can see it hurts my hand. Don't touch me."

The cut I'd given myself in opening the tin of California peaches was bleeding through the dressing and the pain of it reached to my elbow. Flavien seemed disturbed by the wound; he expressed no concern but his eyes darkened as they do when he most desires me. And indeed he's never so amorous as when my teeth chatter with malaria or a spider crab has stung my leg. Suffering, in one already at his mercy, exalts him. His mastery seems the greater; he takes the keener revenge.

"Leave me alone, Flavien. I don't want to be pawed. You know we black people don't go in for *hors d'oeuvres*."

"But you're not really black, Doéllé!" he cried, forgetting that he had implied the contrary a few moments before. "Listen—"

His right eye narrowed. The impatience of his desire gave him the same intense look as on the day he flogged the African workman—the look he had the evening he discovered Urgèle's strange beauty. His voice grew rough, imperious, yet at the same time supplicating. I should have liked Madame Docteur to hear it, for at that moment it was I who dominated Flavien.

"No, Flavien! Among us it's indecent to take off one's clothes to make love."

He responded to my laughter by a hoarse growl, and stripped off my robe—my fine cloth ornamented with hearts and penknives, that counseled me to adorn myself to please. Shadows formed about his eyes and mouth and his voice grew ever more passionate.

"How beautiful you are!" he murmured in my ear. "How I love your breasts—and that pure pubic shell,

61

so trim, so modest. . . . I like the passive way you submit to love, without thinking. Little prehistoric creature —little animal! Yes, you're a little wild animal."

I smiled slightly, waiting. Passive, he called me. A prehistoric creature, a wild animal. And I reflected that white people don't know how to enjoy animal pleasure: they must always mingle with it their mental torments. At the very climax of delight they wrestle with secret thoughts—with regrets and doubts.

No sooner had he released me than he ceased paying me compliments and fell once more a prey to his mysterious suffering. Chill waves washed about him once more. Once more he was an island.

What were his thoughts? Was he working out a scheme to bring Madame Docteur to him, bound and captive? Was he reliving the past that he never spoke of? Little plans, little memories. . . . I never cease to wonder at that pettiness of white people, who have no interests outside their own affairs. With us the individual is secondary to the group. Good and evil, fortunate and unfortunate events, are interesting only in the reactions they awaken in the community; the community indeed imposes obligations on the African, but also guarantees his privileges and ensures his protection.

Meanwhile the afternoon had passed and the abrupt ending of the African day, so depressing to white people, had brought Flavien his cognac and whisky. From under the raised *sekos* I stared fixedly at the mango-bordered road, like Amalia the mulatto contemplating the lagoon. At last darkness fell, and the mating cries of flying foxes—irregular and piercing—began to vibrate round the courthouse.

Flavien was looking desultorily through an old French magazine without paying me the smallest attention. I had become a mere piece of furniture, like the table, the sideboard, or the wicker chair. I rose quietly and walked about in the silence. My hands brushed table, sideboard, and chairs. The wood felt cold. Everything about Flavien radiated cold. His house felt un-lived-in, or as if painful events had taken place there. I never felt at ease in it. Quite ordinary things sent cold shivers down my back: an empty vase, a clock, a carafe. I found myself hunching my shoulders as if the walls had been covered with some noisome substance. Yet all this poison held me prisoner. Flavien chilled me, frightened me, but I could not do without him.

I had paused before a dusty mandolin hanging on the wall, and was looking at the two broken strings. Flavien raised his eyes and followed my glance.

"That mandolin's more than a memory," he said thoughtfully. "It constantly reminds me never to hope."

I was careful not to ask questions, for every time I did he would shut up like an oyster. His voice became aggressive and his look hostile. I had learned to be silent and wait; it was always when I least expected it that he would open a window onto his thoughts. After a moment—I did not know why—he began to speak.

"You can't understand," he said in a very low voice, "but I was an infant prodigy. When I was four my father, who taught the piano, found I had genius. I played scales all day—arpeggios and exercises—until they had to bandage my wrists because of the pain in them. Through the cracks of the window the stench of the slaughterhouse opposite came in. . . . When I drew the curtain I saw rats running along the walls. In the summer the smell was even worse, and there were great bluebottles, too. The daughter of the coppersmith next door—she was fourteen—had heavy breasts and picked up Arabs in the streets. Her mother drank red wine and sang. The slaughterhouse and the coppersmith's house with its grimy windows were my universe as soon as I left the piano. My piano. . . . I worshiped it, and when I played a wrong note it was like a nail driven into my head. Sometimes I would call my father and he'd come and find me in tears. 'It's Beethoven,' I would sob. 'Father, this minor passage is so beautiful it makes me sad.'

"I was six years old and I had a black velvet suit with lace on the collar. People in the casinos and music halls, and people known as the *monde* paid big money to hear me. They all listened uncomfortably and didn't really enjoy my rendering of Liszt. No—they seemed afraid! My father was afraid, too, because I was his chief source of income, and any time I might fall downstairs and sprain my wrist. The doctor said all those headaches of mine might end in meningitis. . . . Now and then Father would say, 'You don't have enough time to play.' He put a little cardboard revolver by the piano and I deserted Bach and Lully—I aimed at a vase and fired, with an Indian war whoop."

Flavien had never talked to me at such length. But it was not to me he spoke; it was to himself. He lit a cigarette, took a gulp of whisky, and went on.

"All our chairs were broken; the cane hung down like unkempt hair and we never had enough money to get them mended. But Father had stuck press cuttings on the walls: a new Mozart, the papers said, and they printed my photograph with eyes too big and hands too small, and showing the system of rods my father had invented to allow my short legs to work the pedals. At seven I composed a tune that became famous. I didn't like my father playing it. 'You play my notes,' I told him, 'but not my feeling.'"

"You're well known in France then, Flavien?" I asked diffidently. He seemed not to hear the question, and went on in an even lower voice.

"Infant prodigies have the choice of two things as a rule: to die or get out. I should have preferred the first, but my opinion wasn't asked, and the new Mozart suddenly became a commonplace performer. The newspapers discovered other prodigies and concert halls closed their doors to me. I tried desperately to be like other little boys, but I never quite managed it: I'd been reared on too many dreams and too much ambition. By the time I was eleven I was talking about the past like an old man; I was already a failure. Now I'm thirty; I feel like the same old man, the same failure."

Flavien rose, his eyes far away. I should have liked him to tell me how he came to choose the profession of colonial magistrate, but he undressed and lay down without another word.

I spent the night with him, unable to sleep for thinking of the little boy he had been. I could so well imagine that little boy in black velvet, sitting at the piano with bandaged wrists and a cardboard revolver in his pocket, his eyes burning with the belief that he would conquer the world. And then that other child rose before me— the child of defeat. The corners of his mouth were turned down in bitterness; he despised his companions because he still felt superior to them, and he began hurting flowers and animals in revenge for not being Mozart.

It was morning.

In all the ramshackle huts women made haste to finish their sweeping before the third cockcrow. Flavien's boy, Amedéwovoé, was roasting coffee in the kitchen.

"*Eso bedo*, Doéllé," he said familiarly.

Amedéwovoé—his name means "some men are good" —had put on airs since enlisting in Gambia and parachuting corned beef to the British in Burma.

"*Eso bedo*, Amedéwovoé!"

I left the courthouse. Flying foxes were hanging upside down in the combretums, like dark coconut shells. A woman in a bright red blanket was standing in the cemetery by a German grave, and a mockingbird sang in the thornbushes.

On arriving at Capitaine Docteur's house I saw

66

Urgèle. She was brushing a black dress on which damp had spread grayish patches, and having hung it in the sun she tossed back her hair and looked at the lagoon. But the lagoon, ringed in its drooping, golden palms, no longer seemed the same.

4

Nynya la adidoé asi métune o.

(Wisdom is as tremendous as the baobab:
no man can encircle it with his arms.)

IT WAS the evening of mail day, and as usual gloom
hung over the station.

For the rest of the week the white people forget that
elsewhere there is civilization—forget the existence of
families, winters, fashions, of a world on the march and
of waiting armies. Sun, alcohol, and quinine make for
listlessness, and people live from day to day without
watch or calendar. The French plane disturbs because
it quickens memory. It renews home ties and sets emo-
tions quivering.

Any letter that comes bears a date already old and is

68

written in bloodless, faded characters by someone with no heart for the task. Soon—one can feel it—one's friends won't be able to write at all. "What's the use?" they'll say. "They're too far away now."

That night, the thirty-first of December, I was in the linen room ironing a black tulle dress for Madame Docteur when Yaya brought the mail. Through the half-open door I saw Urgèle reading her letters. Soon she crumpled the flimsy envelopes and threw herself on the bed, her eyes closed.

"Bad news?" asked Capitaine Docteur in concern, as he slipped off his white overall.

"Not even that," she answered dully. "I don't know —they all talk of snowy streets and holly and skating and dances. No one seems to be thinking of me at all. Are people so soon forgotten when they go away?"

With gestures that were now habitual she dabbed her forehead with a small handkerchief rolled into a ball and threw back her hair.

"And it's too hot here, Frantz. You were quite right —I *am* finding it difficult to get used to Manoho. It's all so heavy. This evening I envy people who can enjoy big fires and feel cold away from them—people who can put on woolen gloves and furs and go walking with a keen, clear mind through the winter wind."

Urgèle's voice had the same plaintive note as on that first morning when she looked at the lagoon. But to avoid emotional scenes and to hide his own feelings the doctor always pretended to attribute certain states of

69

mind to physical causes; he now asked lightly, "Have you been careful to take your quinine these last few days, Urgèle? You seem to me a little feverish."

At this moment I entered the room with the beautiful dress of black tulle which I laid on the bed beside Madame Docteur. She pushed it away crying, "No, Frantz, I'm not feverish. But I don't feel like going out tonight —I don't want to see any of those people again. I've had enough of their mediocrity and vulgarity—their tiredness and their stares and silences and drinking. It hasn't taken me long to find out that colonial life contains all the pettinesses of provincial life multiplied by a hundred."

Capitaine Docteur, who was looking for cuff links in the cupboard, shrugged his shoulders.

"You're hardly off the ship," he said impatiently. "You've done no more than brush the surface of Africa with the tips of your lacquered nails, and you're pronouncing your final judgment on the place. How like a woman!"

Madame Docteur sat up on the bed, crushing the cascades of freshly ironed tulle.

"A woman?" she cried in a sort of despair. "Won't you ever understand—you or anyone else—that it's because I'm not a woman that it's all so frightful?"

"Don't treat me like a woman—I'm not a woman!" She was to repeat this often in the course of those months of fire, dust, and ashes. But who believed her? Capitaine Docteur didn't even listen: he was a matter-

70

of-fact man, incredulous of witchcraft and irritated by the notion of an invisible world. He loved his wife in his own bluff, private fashion, but the enchantment that isolated her from everyday affairs he found exasperating. As for Flavien—Flavien felt at once that he could never reach her; yet to reassure himself he treated her as he treated others, watching her face for the usual reactions; and he soon perceived that with Urgèle he must reckon with the unforeseen. He found her beautiful and attractive; at first he had expected simply to kiss and take her. Yet hardly had he touched her when his arms fell back and fear crept in. For all her fair hair and soft skin Urgèle was not human. He remained hesitant and mute, feeling the barrier between him and the one he loved. "Never," he said to himself, "never shall I be able to snatch her naked from that fascinating sheath, her skin, for she is not in it."

"Don't treat me like a woman!" I seem still to hear that intense voice. Ever since Christmas Eve I had realized that Urgèle was not of this earth and had seen that she found living difficult. She strove to drink and smoke like other women, she feigned to talk their language, but the better part of her was elsewhere. She walked as one dances, with irregular steps, with little surprising leaps and sudden stops. I have never seen anyone else, white or black, walk in that way. It struck me afterward that Madame Docteur was born to fly, like the seagulls. I used to watch the gulls from the Dakar boat. They glided silently, careless of their own flight, turning their beaks listlessly from side to side; dropping suddenly like dead leaves to the breaking seas. Yes, Urgèle was a sea-gull: she hung with slow wingbeats above the swell—she rose surely against the wind—she brushed the stars, but for men she could do nothing. And men could do nothing for her; such was her fate.

That evening I saw her rebel against the power that kept her ever and everywhere in solitude. She rose, scattering crumpled envelopes on the floor, and began to laugh for no reason, with the deep laugh that seemed always to bring tears in its wake. She asked me to fasten her dress; her bare back rose from the full-blown spread of tulle. She had braided her hair about her head and I saw in her eyes a glint of defiance. "Since none of you will understand," they seemed to say, "I'll be a woman this evening. I'll try . . ." Her neck was slender and graceful and she seemed freer and more arrogant than in her other frock—the one she wore at Christmas, that fell to ankle length—and I wondered how she dared appear like this, unadorned by so much as a flower or a necklace; more naked than a statue.

She made herself agreeable to Capitaine Docteur and they went off in the truck to Waji, where the party was being given.

As I meant to go and see my mother I had asked for a lift as far as the experimental nurseries. The three of us sat packed close in the front seat, so that the black tulle skirt covered my green cloth almost completely. I felt as if I were being engulfed in its flounces. I was drowning—stifling— Help!

72

"Why, Doéllé," said Madame Docteur solicitously, "aren't you feeling well?"

I had said nothing. I had made not a sign to betray my distress. But between this white witch and myself vibrations were continually passing, and one of us would often guess what the other was thinking.

"Yes, thank you, perfectly well," I answered, stealthily pushing aside the smothering tulle.

Eyes of the night sparkled in the thickets, phosphorescent and fleeting, keen as the flash of a blade. The headlights swept the gray, smooth trunks of baobab and kapok trees.

"Urgèle's going to meet Flavien—Flavien who in essence resembles her like a brother. Each owes the other a revenge, but which will be the stronger?" I wondered. "*Abobô yi mu gbé a, klo gbo e zê na:* when the snail travels he lodges with the tortoise. I realized this after their first encounter. Each will try to forget, through the other, their common difficulty in living—the secret despair that isolates them. But which of them will go under in the struggle?"

"I hope you'll have an enjoyable evening," I said pleasantly to Madame Docteur as I left her at the nurseries.

I pretended to make for my mother's hut, but hid behind a banyan with tangled, twisted roots that looked like monstrous snakes. One after the other the cars drew up before the house; it was already loud with music; the agricultural officer had brought from Tahiti numerous

73

records of ukulele, guitar, and banjo music. Beneath the raised *sekos* I could see that the walls were decorated with croton flowers and coral lianas; I saw also skirts of green and yellow straw and large conventional photographs of Papeete girls. The artless laugh of the ex-nun reached me; the schoolmaster must have been speaking somewhat freely to her, for in shocked yet delighted tones she murmured, "You shouldn't say things like that to me, Monsieur Marit! You're making me blush."

I had slipped behind the giant anthills, treading the prickly citronella plants, when I heard old Lambert's raucous voice dominating the measured tones of the D.O.; the same words kept recurring in their conversation: "Cassava—falling prices—rising—falling prices . . . Those Syrian scoundrels pirating the coasts—trucks—scales—sacks—cassava—cassava . . ."

As for Madame Elisabeth, she was whispering to the doctor at another window: "My husband loves me desperately. He's obsessed—but I've always been passionately loved. The D.O.'s so jealous that he forbade me to leave my shoulders bare tonight—and that's a pity: I have rather good shoulders." With her blotched hands she drew aside the silk cape that covered her bosom and shamelessly displayed its unmarked skin.

At last I found Flavien and Urgèle; they were standing by the end window, the one opening onto the mandarin trees. She was standing with her back to the *seko* so I couldn't see her face, yet I could feel that her efforts to be like ordinary earthly women had been rewarded. She was almost diabolically seductive. Her head was thrown right back so that her hair brushed the leaves of the mandarins. I could see Flavien; he was saying in a controlled voice: "A star—that's what you are. We all need a star, you know—a star to gaze at in the evenings —if we're to endure life at all. Perhaps we scarcely know its name, and we wonder what manner of world it contains. It is strange and frightening—but it exists and is glorious. But please stay like that! Always be a star. Never become a great burning sun!"

"A great burning sun," she repeated slowly, her bare neck thrown back. "Why not?"

Flavien was taken aback. He had expected a struggle and a volley of words. But this tired voice disconcerted him. Was the rebel surrendering so soon?

"Are you laughing at me?" he demanded incredulously. "You can't know what your coming means in such a wilderness as this. And it would be easy for you to laugh."

"But I'm not laughing," Urgèle assured him. "I never laugh. No one ever taught me how. . . ."

The D.O. was bowing before her and she moved away to dance with him. Flavien lit a cigarette nervously and watched them. The D.O. held Madame Docteur close; he had laid his thin cheek against her hair and was talking to her very eagerly. Flavien stubbed out his cigarette against the wood of the *seko* and walked off abruptly to the other end of the room. The half-extinguished stub that he had thrown out among the mandarins fell on my green blanket, and at that moment a slight rustle near my sandals warned me of a snake; it

75

was sliding unhurriedly toward the kinkilibas: a *serpent-minute*, one of the dread reptiles that bite between the toes. "It's not time to die yet," I thought. "Oh no, not yet. Life's too interesting just now."

I took the path leading to my mother's hut. The rhythmic sighing of ukuleles and banjoes followed me for some moments, but at last silence fell upon the road, and opening my hands to the moonlight I began to breathe deeply.

"Doéllé, what bird dropped you here?"

"Amérique! How are you? Have you been waiting for me?"

"Yes. They told me the doctor's truck had just stopped at the gardens and that you were there in a green blanket."

Amérique, the flat-nosed but finely built native now standing in the middle of the road, was a friend of my childhood; like my mother he belonged to the Ela clan of the Tougba tribe from which the kings of Waji are descended. Lakpan is their fetish, and seeing my friend joyfully hopping about in the moonlight I remembered the great feast of *Ekpan-Chocho* after the *Epé-Ekpé*. All of us, men, women, and children, used to wear old sacks over our blankets for three days, put leaves on our heads, and hide our faces behind yellow painted masks. At that time Amérique was a very lively child; adolescence had not yet solidified and thickened him. I can still see him proudly brandishing a stick adorned with phalli. The inhabitants of Waji formed themselves into a ring, to clap and shout and sing exceedingly indecent songs. I remember how Amérique dragged me in among them to simulate the movements of copulation. But one day the Sisters were angry and carried me off to the Mission. At first my mother looked upon this as an honor and an economy; today I am an educated person, while Amérique still carries a stick as he did during the *Ekpan-Chocho*. Not quite the same sort of stick, of course. The *atikpoé*, as we call it, plays an important part in native life: it's an emblem of authority, an attribute of command. Whether of gold, ivory, or ebony it serves as a visiting card, power of attorney, and passport. Having been appointed stick-bearer to the king of Waji, Amérique fancied himself a person of importance and could not understand my refusal to marry him.

"Let me go, Amérique; the white people might see us, and laugh."

"White people? What do I care for them! Don't you see enough of your magistrate all the rest of the year? Ah, Doéllé, I've missed you. As the proverb says, 'I wore long hair from not seeing you.' It's so long since you came to me. This evening? *Ojé tubé*—you're beautiful. *Moulloô*—I love you! Come—"

"No, no, I must go and see my mother. And anyway I don't want to. Our time of love is over, Amérique!"

Girls, whether Europeanized or not, are free to love where they will. We're quick to take our pleasure before marriage, for once we become a man's legal property our freedom is gone. With us adultery is a crime punishable by law: the Minas put the faithless wife in

77

irons and claim the right to kill the seducer. Our happiest time is when we're single, and Amérique had been one of my whims, nothing more. But he loved me still and desired me.

We walked slowly together through Waji as midnight approached. On all sides the drums resounded in honor of the white people, who were dancing and did not listen.

The ancient town where I was born presented in the moonlight the disorder of a dream; the red mud huts, built higgledy-piggledy here and there according to the humps and hollows of the ground, seemed to overlap one another in a fantastic manner. I was conscious of looming shadows of the unseen. Waji is unlike other places: of its two thousand inhabitants, a thousand are initiates. Where is the thicket, the crossroad, the bridge, or the stream where a fetish does not lurk? Where is the man or woman who would not lay proud claim to some degree of fetishism? The little town is alive with occult powers. Walls whisper, trees implore, earth threatens. What if I do believe in the Jesus of the Christians and make my communion at Easter; each time I come to Waji I'm swept away in a whirlwind of *Sakpate* the smallpox, *Hebiesso* the lightning, *Tokpadoun, Dan*, and other gods as well. On this New Year's Eve dark silhouettes bade me welcome and I recognized the great priestess of the Python Temple, an interpreter of oracles, and a witch. Amérique himself, walking so guilelessly beside me, was possessed of terrible secrets; and I knew that with ravens' feathers, kola nuts, the bile of crocodiles, and the bones of baboons he devised all sorts of amulets, at exorbitant prices. But of this he did not willingly speak, preferring to surround himself with mystery wherever religion and politics were concerned. Nor did he mention the "sworn friends" with whom he had made the blood pact. I dared not ask him about this practice, which was based on the idea that by drinking the blood of a man one is drawn closer to him than a brother. But I knew that one day Amérique would admit to me that two such blood brothers are unconditionally bound to help each other, even for theft—even for murder. He would own to it; meanwhile I was awaiting the favorable moment. I am patient. We Africans are very patient, you see.

We had reached the Snake Temple; my mother lived in a crooked hut just opposite.

"Afutu, Afutu, Afutu . . ."

My mother was a widow, and this word that we heard interminably repeated according to custom was my father's name. For the past six months she had mingled ashes with her food in token of mourning, worn a tattered blanket, and allowed her nails to grow like talons; for such are the observances required of Mina widows.

"Mother, I'm here—Doéllé."

She raised herself on her mat and began weeping.

"Come now, Mother," I said coaxingly, stroking her fat shoulders. "You're tired—that's why you're crying. But in a month your widowhood will be finished; you'll be able to cut your hair and go around thanking your friends for their help during this time. Who knows—perhaps you'll marry again before your elder daughter has chosen a husband for herself!"

From heart-rending groans my mother now broke into helpless laughter. In the eyes of white people we Africans pass with disconcerting abruptness from tears to joy. Amérique and Océa, chatting together under a flamboyant near the hut, also began to cackle with laughter like parrots; nevertheless Amérique exclaimed in a voice tinged with resentment, "You'll have to find a white husband for Doéllé. She has no use for Africans these days."

"Ho, is that true, Doéllé?" demanded my mother anxiously, ready to sob once more; for our happiness and grief play hide and seek with one another like children. Amérique had spoken the truth. I had no use for Africans. This hut in which I'd grown up, naked among pythons and clay fetishes, had become alien to me. This woman, my mother, a slave to obsolete tradition—what could she do for me? That night I strove in vain to recapture the charm of the past; my spirit yearned toward a house hung with coral lianas and lulled by a new music. Drinking palm wine with Amérique and Océa I thought of the champagne that Flavien and Urgèle would be enjoying in the gardens. And a shudder of painful excitement ran through me at the thought of soon being back among the white people—the white people who hurt me so and shut me out of their parties.

Soon the first cockcrow was heard.

"I must go now, Mother. Beside you the night has passed quickly and sweetly. I'll come back."

Already I was outside, longing to run.

"Stay with me, Doéllé!" pleaded Amérique, all desire.

"Afutu, Afutu, Afutu . . ." whined my mother, alone once more.

"Soon!" cried Océa, from where she stood beneath the flamboyant.

When I reached the white people's bungalow, all the little girls of Waji, dressed in their gorgeous best, were running about the gardens waving handkerchiefs. They caught one another by the hand, formed a ring right around the bungalow, and sang at the tops of their voices in the growing light: "*Allé lé ô!* Joy, welcome, and a happy New Year! *Allé lé ô!*"

One of them uttered a shrill musical phrase that was taken up enthusiastically by her companions amid the frenzied waving of handkerchiefs; another voice followed, more piercing still, and the distant drums resounded in answer. Fetish priestesses approached along the citronella walk; they were grave, full of things unspoken, and their cowrie shells slipped like rosaries between their tattooed breasts. They prostrated themselves in greeting before the D.O., who threw handfuls of coin to them and to the little girls. The clamor became general when the chiefs made their dignified appearance, bringing white fowls, bottles of wine wrapped in purple scarves, pineapples, green oranges, and huge bunches of frangipani.

81

"*Allé lé ô!*" chorused the little girls once more as they turned homeward.

It was almost day when we climbed into the truck, Madame Docteur and I. Urgèle's face seemed washed of color and she looked exhausted by the woman's part she had played that night. She leaned a little against my shoulder and I saw that she was sleeping; she looked so appealing that I had to stifle an impulse to protect her as if she'd been a child.

"Are you going to let your enemy touch your heart?" I said to myself severely. "Come now, no weakening! Summon up your strength; soon you will have need of the most burning hatred."

5

Nku kpo azi mu du azi wo.

(The eye that stares at the groundnut
does not eat it.)

INDEED, but for the image of Flavien that stood
between us, I could have been almost fond of Urgèle.
I still hoped that she would represent for him the inaccessible white woman to be admired from a distance,
that he might the better appreciate my dark skin. Men
who live with African women all dream of some impossible love that will rouse them from the lethargy into
which they sink by contact with us; this need of escape
is so acute that at times they invent passions for themselves. Life at the station is very restricted and the
intimacy among the white people compulsory and un-
broken. In every official's house a bored woman is to be

found; she it is who comes to be credited with qualities she lacks. Her pettiness is ignored with a kind of desperation by men who force themselves to believe that she is wonderful and swear they are in love. There are men like Flavien who store up dreams for years until they're in a chronic state of expectation and watchfulness, ready to pounce.

"Let's hope," I thought, "that Urgèle will be no more to Flavien than a source of dreams, as she is—thanks to her black dresses and her scent—for the cassava planter, the schoolmaster, the D.O., and the agricultural officer. Let's hope I shan't have to resort to fetishes."

And even if they had wanted to meet alone at the courthouse, how could they manage it? Take what precautions they might, there would always be some boy, some *mousso*, to espy Madame Docteur leaving the place; and before the hero and heroine had time to put up their defenses the whole station would be whispering. There are indeed husbands who, exhausted by the climate, are content for a young bachelor to relieve them of their conjugal obligations; such men make matters easy by punctual absences during which the faithless wife may receive her lover beneath her own roof without fear. Luckily for me, Capitaine Docteur could never be numbered among these meek men. On the contrary, I had seen enough of his hasty temper to know that in such a case he would be quite unyielding.

"Everything's all right. I'm happy. I shall keep Flavien." I repeated this to myself every day, knowing that by affirmation we can bring about what we most desire.

But late one afternoon Capitaine Docteur set off for the Amegnodan dispensary, and shortly afterward I saw Urgèle coming down the steps of their bungalow. I ceased to believe that all was going so well. Something disturbing and excited in her manner made me look up from registering the birth of twins, Akuele and Akoko. This was an event, for twins are honored here; they're said to leave their human shell at night to become red monkeys, and if these are killed by some hunter the babies die at the same instant. But what did I care for Akuele and Akoko at that moment? Madame Docteur in her violet frock was taking the road to the cemetery.

"Amavi," I said to the second nurse, "take my place for a moment. I must go out now, but I shall soon be back."

I followed Madame Docteur's uneven dancing steps. It was not the first time she had been to the cemetery; I had taken her there the day after Christmas and she had come back quite depressed. But now I could not recognize the woman who had wandered so tearfully among the ruined tombs, brushing with her fingers the half-effaced names on the headstones. She was no longer afraid of snakes in the thornbushes, it seemed, for behind a Portuguese tomb with rose-colored pillars someone was waiting for her.

Their greeting was hasty and uneasy. Flavien glanced about the expanse of graves and paper garlands as if wondering where they could hide. Then he shrugged his shoulders slightly and took Madame Docteur by the arm.

85

Skirting the scarlet mounds and the crosses with their English inscriptions—"Departed this Life to Life Eternal"—I followed the couple toward the sea. I followed from one coconut palm to the next; the leaves, faint with drought, swayed on the stems and seemed to be spying too, and listening.

They walked side by side but their hands no longer touched; although no one ever came to the cemetery they felt uneasy. Flavien knew that white people are always under the observation of unseen eyes, and he turned his head from side to side as he went.

"You seem preoccupied," said Madame Docteur reproachfully. "You weren't like this at the nurseries."

"I wouldn't want any trouble to come to you through me," he said solicitously. "You don't know what it's like. Here in Manoho one's never alone. To a newcomer like you the Africans just seem a remote crowd whose faces are all alike, don't they? But the native labels each white person carefully, watches his reactions, notes his movements, and repeats his most innocent remarks."

"Surely you're exaggerating," said Urgèle impatiently. "You colonials make such a fuss about nothing. Why should we care what the natives like or don't like? Haven't we the right to go for a walk alone together?"

"No. And you know it."

They had reached the extreme end of the cemetery where it borders on the beach. Never had the boom of the surf along the bar sounded to me so heavy. They stood one behind the other under the drooping palms, waiting for the light to fade; but the day, as if wishful to keep them waiting, would not end. From tree trunk to tree trunk I drew near, watching, listening.

Suddenly Flavien seized Urgèle by the shoulder and shaking her in a sort of fury he said, "I hate seeing you furtively like this, having to talk to you with six or seven other people there—always the same ones—or else having to meet you here in a cemetery and jump at every sound. Don't you feel how impossible it is? We simply cannot go on like this any longer, Urgèle!"

She replied lightly at first; she played the part of a woman and said what any white woman would have said to so urgent a plea from such a quarter.

"But, Flavien, you must be used to life out here! You must know how to control yourself in front of eight people—how to be patient and spend a week in planning a walk in the cemetery. Was your life any different at your other stations—at Wagadugu or Kankan?"

"I don't know. I've forgotten. *You're* here, Urgèle. I have no memories, I can make no comparisons—no choice even!"

Around them the palms made a rustling sound as of rain.

"Is it raining?" asked Madame Docteur quickly.

"No, no—it's only the palm trees."

"If you're quite sure—" she stammered, distracted because Flavien was looking at her mouth and saying fiercely, "Urgèle, I can't forget you. At night I imagine you and in the daytime I talk to you. Can you hear my secret words—the words I've kept within me for years? I don't know how to speak them."

"I can guess. . . . Especially in the mornings when I wake—before my defenses are up. Yes, then I hear them."

He drew her against his shoulder, the scarred shoulder that had been my property for nearly two years. The palm trees enveloped them in their rustling canopy: Flavien was kissing Urgèle. But he did not shut his eyes as when he kissed me; with me he sought who knows what image behind his lowered lids. No, his gaze pierced the curtain of palm leaves as if he had sensed my presence.

The trunk that concealed me was crawling with busy ants. A lizard with an orange tail came down to the level of my face and rose on its little elbows to observe me curiously. At that moment a piece of bark cracked under my foot.

"We must go," said Flavien abruptly, and he drew away from Madame Docteur. His eyebrows were drawn together as on his worst days, and cold waves washed around him once more.

"What's the matter?" asked Urgèle, mechanically smoothing her fair hair.

"Nothing. But we'd better get out of the cemetery."

"Already?"

"Yes."

Urgèle, disappointed, shook out her violet frock. No doubt she was reflecting that this romantic walk among the graves was not without its hazards. "We shall have a long, quiet talk," she probably had hoped. "Flavien will say all the words that my husband doesn't know, and he'll be tender as Frantz has never known how to be. Flavien I know will understand me. Perhaps he's not like other men, having lived so long alone. He'll soothe and console me and I shall find the peace I've been vainly seeking for so many years."

Urgèle, foolish Urgèle! You knew that no man could ever understand, soothe, or console you! You knew that never in this life could you find that longed-for peace.

Flavien lit a cigarette as they moved silently among the graves. A coconut smashed heavily on the broken column of a German tomb. Night was falling at last, but too late. Night was falling on the graves but not on lovers' kisses. "Who sows the wind shall reap the whirlwind." "Departed this Life to Life Eternal." "*Auf Wiedersehen. Auf Wiedersehen.*"

"You know," said Flavien in a jerky voice, "there are times when I wonder how people can exist in such places as this. I can't even walk home with you. Go back to the hospital by the road. We'll meet again soon, though I don't know how or where. I'll think of something—I'll find something and soon we'll be alone together, Urgèle."

Darkness fell swiftly. Flavien's eyes followed Urgèle as she took the road to the hospital; then he made for the courthouse. I returned to the maternity clinic through the night-filled cemetery.

Before dinner I went to see Urgèle, having made sure that Capitaine Docteur was not yet back from the bush dispensary. I wanted to gloat a little over her discomfiture, and by way of pretext I took her a bunch of jasmine mixed with red ixoras. She was lying on the little divan on the veranda, and her features were rigid. I held out the bouquet but she threw the innocent flowers roughly down beside her.

"Forgive me, Doéllé," she said quickly. "I feel so nervous this evening. Seven o'clock is the worst time for me here. How I envy you, Doéllé—how I envy you your inward and outward serenity. I'm always either on the heights or in the depths and it exhausts me. And this time of day's so depressing. I'm beginning to see why everyone in Manoho drinks so much before dinner."

Yaya was just setting down a tray of shining glasses, cognac, and iced water.

"White people do say," I remarked softly, "that at seven o'clock one feels the full weight of the day—the weight of all the things left undone, unfinished. . . ."

She threw me a quick, searching glance and I thought she was going to ask me a question; but she lay back against the faded cotton cushions and remained silent. I watched her. She had removed the violet frock and now wore an indoor dress of white crepe with wide, floating sleeves. She was lovely, unquestionably lovely.

I looked at her. I regretted my ignorance of witchcraft and was sorry indeed not to have asked Amérique for a powerful *grigri*. Yet I've been taught that concentrated thought is strong enough to turn aside a tornado or an army on the march, and so I bent my mind upon Urgèle:

"*Give him up, Madame Docteur! Listen, there's still*

time—you can forget. Remember, a love that can't flow freely, a love nourished on vain hopes, brings shame with it. Guilt will gather round you like a swarm of black ants. No more carefree mornings on the lagoon; your freedom—vanished! You're already deaf and dumb to life—you would become more so. Everything would be stirred up and muddied—and for what? You know that unseen powers have destined you to loneliness and vestal purity."

Such were the thoughts that I directed upon Madame Docteur; and I know that, once sent forth, thought multiplies and radiates independently of the sender, traveling by unsuspected magnetism. "Thoughts thus stressed, ever reformulated and repeated, must have their effect," I told myself. "At every hour of the day I must separate Urgèle from Flavien. Every hour until I succeed."

Urgèle, her head thrown back on the cushions, seemed to answer with full understanding: "Yes, you're right, Doéllé. I'll keep away from Flavien."

Did I not say that she and I were linked by a sort of continuous telepathy?

At last she raised her head as if roused from sleep and said in surprise, "Why, are you still here? I thought you'd gone back to the hospital. Thank you for your flowers, Doéllé. You're so charming!"

She made an effort to smile, and stroked my bare shoulder with a rather feverish hand.

"Your skin's as soft as the wing of a flying fox," she said. I went down the steps, smiling too.

Would you have thought me so charming, Madame Docteur, if I'd told you that this shoulder—soft as the wing of a flying fox, you said?—was all Flavien's? Would you indeed have thought me charming?

6

Ne lakle melé afe o la, ye dzogolo zua dzata.

(When the leopard's away the civet cat becomes a lion.)

A FEW DAYS later we went off on tour. Capitaine Docteur, Madame Docteur, and I were in the leading truck, with Kankwe the cook and the boy Yaya, who with difficulty kept our load of canned provisions from toppling over. The second truck followed close behind, bringing the leprosy specialists, the census officer, the interpreter, the assistants who carried vaccine in hollowed lengths of bamboo, and lastly Mamidou the policeman proudly bearing his rifle. Two whites and eleven Africans. We expected to be away for a week.

Madame Docteur had begged to come with her husband.

"I don't want to let you go, Frantz," she said. "We've been apart for two years and it's a bad thing for us to get the habit of being alone. When we married, on your last leave, we had only six months to get to know each other; and this time we still haven't quite met. We mustn't let the gap between us widen. Don't let's ever leave each other again, Frantz!"

He had made no reply. A sudden flush followed by pallor swept over his rugged face; I knew that Urgèle's words had struck home, and disquieted him perhaps. But Madame Docteur who had turned and was thoughtfully gazing over the lagoon, failed to notice these revealing signs. She awaited the comfort of words and was hurt by his silence. Nevertheless the doctor gave orders for another camp bed to be put in the truck, and so we started.

"She's afraid to stay in Manoho alone," I thought at first. "She's afraid that Flavien might call to see her. She clings to her husband as to a lifebuoy—she's obeying my silent order to forget the walk in the cemetery. All is well and I'm happy—as happy as I was before the killing of the python."

But instead of rejoicing I should have done better to remain on my guard, strengthen my powers, and remember that a slain python is never balked of its vengeance. But what woman can boast of never having succumbed to the intoxication of triumph?

I was lively and cheerful when we arrived at Kpandamé, on the banks of the river. It was our first village. The chief had caused a great tent of woven palm leaves—the *apatam*—to be raised in the square, and on all sides the gongs resounded to summon the people. They poured in along every track, wearing their gala blankets, and assembled patiently beneath the *apatam* until the time came to file past the doctor. Somewhat to one side, near the assistants and their microscopes, I began weighing the babies; but I could see Capitaine Docteur sitting between Madame Docteur and the interpreter, and I heard all they said.

"This man calls himself Major, this one Governor, and that other one End-of-the-Month," explained the doctor to Urgèle, who plied him unceasingly with questions. "It's not so easy to make a census: they change their names when they're ill to throw the evil spirits off the scent. As for their age, they either don't know it or deliberately skip a few years. 'I've forgotten,' that woman says, 'I've quite forgotten.'"

"Wonderful!" said Urgèle in her grave voice.

"Think so? There speaks the Parisian. Don't you see how difficult all this vagueness makes our work? Come on, Sossou, show us your leg."

The eyes of Madame Docteur which had never before glanced at anything that had not been censored, sifted, and refined, now fell upon the deeply hollowed purple sores of syphilis, upon weeping ulcers and gigantic boils. Yet I must own she didn't turn away her head when they brought a child with a growth the size of an orange on its forehead, hollowed away inside in bleed-

95

ing corruption. Without blenching she beheld an ankle swollen and split on which a ball of white thread seemed to have been grafted. Capitaine Docteur prescribed a hot permanganate dressing. Being a colonial doctor of ten years' standing and therefore accustomed to suppurating diseases he did not even notice that his wife had turned pale.

I had finished weighing the infants and was persuading a young mother not to drown her baby; it was hydrocephalic and the weeping woman declared that she could not survive three moons after the birth of this deformity. Her loud sobs prevented me from following the conversation at the other table, and I silenced the woman with a blow of my fist on the scales.

"For all these people," Capitaine Docteur was saying, "illness is simply the expression of anger on the part of a fetish, and so they think it's useless to guard against malaria, syphilis, yaws, or leprosy. No one can defy the will of the spirits. Africans aren't very sensitive to physical pain so long as they can see its cause. That case of yaws there—green and yellow with suppuration as you can see—laughs gaily at the sight of you and your white skin. That young boy with the shoulder wound is perfectly happy. But a patient like the woman you see there on the left in the green turban always looks gloomy. Her illness is invisible, you see; she has pains in her head."

A young girl now presented herself before the doctor. She wore a brilliant cloth with a pattern of golden yellow birds, but on her back was a large, uneven, pink-ish patch.

"Leprosy. Usual treatment."

Urgèle shrank a little; perhaps she feared to catch the disease through merely looking at it.

"The girl's smiling," remarked the doctor. "Her ill-ness can be seen, so she's quite content, and worries no more than you do when you break a fingernail."

Beneath the *apatam* that threw a delicate play of light and shade on the ground, Capitaine Docteur seemed to me relieved, even cheerful. He was evidently glad to have Urgèle beside him. "If she's really going to take an interest in my job she shall come everywhere with me," he seemed to be thinking. "Let her give up her dreamy nonsense and come down to earth, and we shall be a united pair at last." To entertain his wife he went on talking, though he had little love for words.

"Later on I'll take you north. You'll see whole vil-lages there whose inhabitants are without toes or fin-gers—they have faces like lions' and their eyes are red. The difficulty is to make them understand how serious leprosy is; they can't see the point of chaulmoogra oil injections. At first out of mere curiosity they come to see our assistants, and then they forget all about it. Because of this, many doctors have arranged with the D.O.s that sensible patients who attend the bush dis-pensary regularly shall be exempted from taxation. Would you like to come north with me soon?"

"Yes, Frantz, I'll come with you," said Madame Doc-

97

teur eagerly, thinking perhaps: "By then I shall have quite forgotten Flavien. In fact I've begun to forget him already. I haven't missed him so much these last few days, and this morning I've only thought about him three times. All I must do now is close my ears so as not to hear him calling to me when I wake in the mornings."

At midday we all three gathered at the chief's hut. He had a bottle of apéritif uncorked in our presence, and to convince the white people that he did not mean to poison them he rinsed each glass with the vermouth and afterward swallowed the tepid rinsings. We drank in silence, after the chief had poured a little on the ground in homage to his ancestors.

Heat weighed upon the village. The chief languidly waved his fly whisk. Capitaine Docteur said how glad he was that sleeping sickness was decreasing in our district, to which the chief ceremoniously replied that it was thanks to the courage and tenacity of white doctors that the tsetse fly no longer did as much damage as formerly. Urgèle looked through the window at the sparkling river, while I looked at her. She must have felt my eyes fixed upon her, for now and then she turned her head inquiringly, as if uneasy.

"All is over between you and the magistrate, Madame Docteur. Finished, finished."

That is what I was saying to her with all my strength. Every living being possesses this power: gods, men, beasts, and things. Only the degree varies. How can the white people laugh at our convictions and ignore the most important factor in life: the thing that determines laughter and tears, that can wound or protect, save or destroy? Every moment we Africans use these individual powers, increasing and intensifying them.

I felt sure of my power over Urgèle that day. I believed I had won, and unhappily for myself I ceased sending these silent orders to my rival.

"Well, Doéllé—in the clouds? What are you thinking about so hard? Poor company for a sane, balanced man: a wife who never comes down to earth, and a daydreaming nurse. Come along, now, hurry! The chief tells me there are hippopotamus only a mile and a half away, and I'd like to have a shot at them after lunch."

The doctor was shaking my arm and joking. He was in great good humor that day; I had never seen him like this before. We went to lunch. The chief had put the best hut in the village at our disposal. It was decorated with a heart and a hand of painted clay. Kankwe was awaiting us with a penitent air, having spilt paraffin in the butter and Madame Docteur's scent in the quinine.

"I forgive you this time," said Capitaine Docteur. He was indeed in an exceptionally forbearing and cheerful mood.

We ate in silence. Outside, the village lay crushed beneath the sun. A black horde had taken possession of the openings of the hut, blocking what little air might be hoped for beneath its low roof. Inquisitive eyes, white teeth, smothered laughter, whispering . . . A baby made so bold as to come and touch Madame Docteur's skin; then looked at its finger with an air of surprise, as if expecting to see white paint on it. At this there was more and louder laughter.

Urgèle, as I could feel, was breathing with difficulty; she was in need of air. She put her hand between her slip and her breast and opened her mouth slightly; yet she was ready to endure heat and the sight of yaws and leprosy the better to forget Flavien. With a momentary feeling of pity I rose and with a forward sweep of my arms scattered the murmuring crowd. The children fled in a fright and air entered the cramped hut once more. Urgèle drew a breath and looked at me gratefully. But already the girls and children were back at their observation posts, blocking all openings with the compact mass of their naked bodies.

"Isn't there any more water in the thermos bottles?" asked Urgèle. "The stuff in the cans is so warm. Frantz, would you ask Yaya to open a coconut for me?"

"There, what did I say!" exclaimed Capitaine Docteur. "Didn't I tell you the day after you came that you'd get to like it?"

To like it . . . It's true that from that day onward Urgèle was so fond of coconut milk that she drank a glass of it every morning at Manoho. Indeed it was because of this— But not yet. The time has not yet come to talk of that.

All that day Madame Docteur's temples throbbed and her heart beat like a bell, but she would not show it. I reflected that she must be delicate, as the least fatigue hollowed her cheeks, and that it was this fragile look that despite my hatred made me want to protect her.

"Feeling tired out, Urgèle?" asked Capitaine Docteur. "I warned you these trips aren't very restful. Go and have a quiet siesta; Doéllé will look after you, and I'll go after the hippopotamus with Mamidou."

"No, Frantz, I'm perfectly all right. I'll come with you," she said, with the half-smile that was both mocking and sad. "Hippopotamus! I've never seen any except in the films."

Anything to avoid being alone during the hours of heat that induce thought—to avoid seeing in the khaki folds of the mosquito net that tormented, ravaged face; hearing a voice in her ear murmuring, "I don't know—I've forgotten. You're here, Urgèle. There are no memories, no comparisons—no choice even!"; feeling on one's lips a certain kiss . . . Anything to avoid these things.

But by the river the heat was almost unbearable, and the brown waters blazed. Two naked girls were washing on the shore, rubbing themselves with the coconut fiber that makes the skin so soft. Soft as the wing of a flying fox, Madame Docteur!

Silence. The pirogue glided first to the right, then to the left, then to the middle of the stream; the boatmen knew the river well and how to dodge the sandbanks. Madame Docteur shifted her sun helmet continually; she bathed her legs with the thick river water and readjusted her dark glasses, feeling terrible faintness from the oppressive heat. I was sitting bareheaded in the stern and I turned my face to the sun that she so dreaded. This sky was made for *us*, Madame Docteur, not for white women like you. The banks slid greenly by, and from time to time one could hear the cry of a monkey or the melodious notes of a Senegal dove. Three egrets on a rosy beach watched us as we passed; their plumage was spotlessly white.

"Look out—there they are! Steady now!" came Capitaine Docteur's whispered order to the boatmen. Between thirty and forty yards away appeared the creatures' ears, absurdly, touchingly pink above the massive bodies. They blew a cloud of water and dived. There were three of them. They played for a moment in the heart of the river and reappeared placidly farther on. There followed a deafening report.

"Missed!" exclaimed Capitaine Docteur disgustedly.

"Oh, Frantz, how I loathe that noise!" Madame Docteur's hands were still pressed to her ears.

"You should be thankful you didn't kill one of them," I said half seriously. "The python at Christmas was quite enough."

"But the hippopotamus isn't a fetish animal so far as I know."

"Yes and no. Anyhow it's a vindictive one, and always takes revenge on the hunter who kills it. My uncle Gamélé killed one once, and afterward when he was coming back very proud to his hut he met a poor old man who begged food and shelter of him. He couldn't refuse, for often these travelers are fetishes, testing people's generosity. And so the old man slept in my Uncle Gamélé's hut; but at dawn he went mad and killed my uncle's eldest son with a hatchet. So you see the hippopotamus lost no time in manifesting his wrath."

"Then I can only rejoice at being such a bad shot," remarked Capitaine Docteur. "But it's time for me to get back to my patients. Before joining me at the *apatam*, Doéllé, will you take my wife to see the market?"

At the market they sold pimento, little heaps of salt on teak leaves, clay pipes, and red beads. A woman I knew hailed me; she was carrying a tray on her head on which were laxative pills, little bottles of cognac, aphrodisiacs, statuettes from Lourdes, and panthers' whiskers for amulets.

"Ho!" I said severely. "The Blessed Virgin among *grigris?* Aren't you ashamed?"

She tapped me merrily on the shoulder.

"Doéllé! You know that for us the Virgin is just another fetish, like St. Joseph and Jesus."

Urgèle smiled when I translated this, and her eyes followed the woman who was now chatting with a *gombo* seller.

"She's beautiful," she said, "and she walks better than a Parisian mannequin. Tell me, Doéllé, what do white men think of native women? I'd be interested to know."

"Some men pretend to despise them when they talk about them in the towns, but when they go on trips they find them irresistible. Others live with natives and afterward take no interest in white women."

The smells, colors, and cackle of the market made us dizzy. I guided Madame Docteur unobtrusively to a place apart against a wall where only a *tolegba*—a clay fetish—with a fierce wooden phallus could overhear us.

Madame Docteur removed her sun helmet and asked slowly, reluctantly, "Do you know any white men in Manoho who are in love with native women?" She wanted to know and was afraid to learn.

"That's an awkward question. Must I answer?"

"Yes—I want to know."

I answered only because she insisted. "They say that Madame Elisabeth's husband is greatly interested in his little pupils, and that *le père* Lambert, in spite of his age—"

She looked at me strangely. "And the magistrate?"

"Must I answer?" I said, twisting a corner of my blanket in feigned embarrassment.

"Yes, please—I want you to."

I plunged. "The magistrate likes native women. He even says he can't do without them."

I reveled in the pallor that overspread her features. So sensitive was she that the smallest emotion was reflected in her face.

"But when did he tell you that, Doéllé? And do you mean really primitive natives, like that woman selling statuettes of the Virgin? He wasn't speaking of half-Europeanized girls—girls who know how to think—girls like—?"

Her gaze pierced me through and through. She had

retreated two steps and her leg brushed the erected organ of the fetish.

There was no need for me to answer; she had understood. Didn't we always understand one another? I just smiled. She repressed a cry of amazement and jealousy and quickly replacing her helmet she ran back toward the *apatam*.

"Good idea," I thought without moving. "Seek refuge with Capitaine Docteur. You'll need consolation after so painful a discovery. Now you know that Flavien and I are one and that when we meet it's not in a cemetery. This knowledge will help you to chase an evening's illusion from your mind."

I felt relieved of a great weight. Around me the life of the village flowed peacefully. Men were hollowing a pirogue from the trunk of a kapok tree; others were weaving mats and hurdles of bamboo. The fires that Capitaine Docteur had ordered for the burning of garbage began to leap up on all sides. Women, their pitchers upside down on their heads, were going to the river for water.

"All is well. For me all is well. I'm happy."

Green pigeons settled on the fig trees and night fell. The woman in the market had invited me to dine with her; we had smoked *agouti* and yam paste. Then we went and listened to the storyteller in the market place. The tale seemed endless: hospitality and cunning were extolled, stupidity and greed ridiculed. Which acted most wisely, the goat or the elephant? Had the hyena second sight? The storyteller questioned his hearers, each of whom sought to shine by the acuteness of his answers. Little chance though Africans may have of becoming engineers and mathematicians in the world of the future, they will make notable lawyers. They can stick to an idea and defend it.

Meanwhile the thread of the story had been lost sight of, and when I left they were heatedly discussing a proverb which had nothing to do with the theme: *"To vi gblô be: eza do! Novi gblo be: zô mi yi, nu ke le za me?* The consanguine brother says, 'It is night.' The uterine brother says, 'Let us go. What is there in the night?'"* And they plunged into anecdotes of quarrels, scenes of jealousy and even crime between half brothers and half sisters born of different mothers.

"Let's go! What is there in the night?" I repeated to myself. "Let's go and see whether Capitaine Docteur and Urgèle have got to proverbs yet, in the hut adorned with a heart and a hand."

But they can have found little to say to one another, for they were already in bed. Shunning the airless heat of the hut they had had their camp beds set up in the compound, and the black mob that at noon had crowded to watch them eat now ran up on padding feet to see them sleep. The round, dazzling moon lit up the vague forms under the mosquito net. Madame Docteur was certainly troubled in her mind, for she turned this way and that unable to find oblivion; she must have been imagining our meetings—Flavien's and mine—in the big room at the courthouse, and our untroubled, carefree kisses. Nervously she slapped at the insects buzzing within the mosquito netting; she covered her face with the sheet to escape the cruel light of the moon; and at last I saw her sit up on the thin mattress, scared by the golden specks that whirled hither and thither like mad stars. And they were only fireflies.

The bass notes of the bullfrog dominated the stridency of the crickets. In the distance, the far distance, a hyena laughed.

"Good morning, Doctor! Did you sleep well, Madame?"

It was morning. I had just bathed in the river and felt fresh and rested. Seated on her bed from which she had pushed back the mosquito net, Urgèle was staring drearily in front of her. Her features had changed; they were those of one pursued by care even in sleep. She refused Kankwe's coffee, but drank coconut milk from the green shell. Not far away Capitaine Docteur, stripped to the waist, toweled himself vigorously and looked the picture of health and strength.

All seemed new that morning—airy and joyous: sky, river, colors, smells, and creatures. Urgèle alone was lifeless and sad, and stared blindly at the cracked mud wall from which fetish bones peeped out. On the right were two tobacco plants in flower; on the left a goatskin was drying, already buzzing with flies, while in the middle of the compound rose a shapeless fetish, red with the blood of that same goat.

"We're in the heart of fetish country," I told Madame Docteur carelessly. "Would you like to come with me? At the entrance to the village I'll show you the protector of warriors and hunters: *Gu*, the bloodthirsty. And *Tolegba* who carries a disemboweled animal on his clay chest, and *Ho*, who eats children."

Urgèle drew farther along the bed and looked at me with a hatred of which I should not have thought her capable. But before she could answer me my hands fell to my sides in amazement.

Flavien was there. He stood beside the tobacco plants in the old khaki shorts that he keeps for treks in the bush. He must have come in at the back, unseen, and there was something unreal and rather frightening about his appearance among us. Sometimes he would remark with a smile, "I don't look much like a magistrate, do I?" but this morning he looked the perfect judge. Perhaps he had sensed from afar that I had wounded Urgèle and was making ready to do her further harm, and had hurried to her defense.

He shook hands with Capitaine Docteur, who also looked surprised by this unexpected visit.

"I had some business to see to at Kpandamé," Flavien explained briefly. "I knew you were still here so I thought I'd come. How's everything? I must see the chief—is he about?"

But to Madame Docteur his eyes were shouting: "It's not true! I didn't have to come to Kpandamé or see the chief. I had to see you. So many days have passed since our walk in the cemetery and you'll be away for another week. Have you forgotten me? I couldn't wait any longer—I had to know at once whether you'd forgotten me. Tell me!"

She had quickly slipped on a wrap and risen; behind her the mosquito net trailed like a soiled, crumpled bridal veil. She looked reproachfully at Flavien. "Why have you come?" said her eyes. "I was forgetting you, yes! And now you've come to throw my thoughts into a turmoil again."

I was thinking: "He must have left Manoho last night to reach Kpandamé so early, and yet he hates driving at night. When a man forgets his natural selfishness it's time to open one's eyes. Things are getting serious."

Capitaine Docteur had gone off to his consultations in the *apatam* and the three of us were left together, Urgèle, Flavien, and I. No one spoke.

It was he who broke the silence at last.

"Here's a thermos," he said to Madame Docteur. "I thought that after your first day in the bush you might be glad of some iced *menthe*."

I disappeared charitably into the hut, so great was their need to talk to each other alone. But from within I allowed myself to ask the man I loved, "Are you staying here tonight, Flavien?"

What more natural than this question? Madame Docteur knew about us, though she must surely have whitened at the familiar *tu* with which I addressed him. The reply was slow in coming, and rather feeble.

"It's court day tomorrow. I shall start for Manoho almost at once."

So Flavien was afraid I should make a scene. He dared

not push me out of the way deliberately, and was being cautious. My voice grew tender, almost wifely.

"May I help you pack your case?"

"No!" The word was barked rather than spoken. In two strides he had joined me in the hut; he seized my wrist and twisted it and I thought he was going to strike me. In the compound I saw Madame Docteur turning away and wondered why she looked so ashamed.

I managed to free my wrist and moved away toward the bamboo screen that concealed an improvised shower. I moved slowly, dragging my feet like Amalia the mulatto. There was no need for me to take a shower, as I'd bathed in the river at dawn; yet I undressed and dashed water over myself with a cracked calabash. I emerged dripping, and without troubling to dry myself I appeared as I was, with my blanket over my arm, before the two who had taken refuge in the hut.

"I haven't got a towel," I said. "Lend me yours, Flavien, will you?" And without waiting for an answer I took one from his open case, also some lavender water, and began tranquilly rubbing myself down before them. There were no chairs in the hut; Urgèle and Flavien stood watching me in silence. A mason wasp buzzed round and round behind them against the uneven wall and the slight noise filled the hut—filled our ears because of the silence that hung over us. Flavien's right eye had narrowed until it was no more than a slit through which gleamed a murderous light, yet with unhurried movements I resumed my blanket. That wasp was really maddening! One could hear nothing else. Life seemed at a standstill and the wasp buzzed on.

"Leave us, Doéllé."

What a world of contempt was in that tone, what disgust in his look! "Charming behavior," he seemed to be saying, "from a black girl who claims to be the equal of whites! Is this the way to win respect?" The corners of his mouth were turned down and his repressed fury made him almost ugly. Smiling, I went out.

I could safely leave them alone together. They were in no mood now for words of love. Madame Docteur, outraged by my indecent performance, would not fail to attack Flavien.

"It was disgraceful of you, Flavien! You should have told me at the beginning that that woman—"

"I know, I know, Urgèle, my dear—but really it's so unimportant. All the men here are in more or less the same situation. Africans don't count."

"Until yesterday I regarded Doéllé as having intelligence and decent feeling, and being more interesting than many white women. What is she to you?"

"Nothing, nothing. A graceful little creature in my empty bungalow."

Dear Flavien! But what did it matter what he said of me? He thought he meant it, and I was easy in my mind. I could go away without misgivings, for they would not kiss. The poison was working. There were also the chief's wives grinding corn and kneading dough in the compound, and they would not fail to keep an eye on Capitaine Docteur's wife.

The doctor finished his consultations during the worst of the heat. The last patients returned home and the assistants put away their microscopes. That afternoon we should be able to take the big pirogues and move on to Agbalafin and install ourselves beneath another *apatam*. The magistrate, thank heaven, would be on his way to Manoho and we should be relieved of his burdensome presence.

"Doéllé, where have you been all this time? You know, you've been slacking lately; you're not the efficient nurse I knew a year ago. It's depressing how all you Africans lack perseverance. I've been waiting for you here for ten minutes to see that difficult confinement case, and you've made me late. See that it doesn't happen again."

The doctor had lost his good humor of yesterday. His fingers drummed on the table as he spoke—we were in the *apatam*—and the powerful jaw muscle quivered. We went. He spoke not another word, and I wondered whether he was really angry with me or whether it was the magistrate's coming that had irritated him. We found the woman unconscious. Around her, relations were invoking their ancestors, burning black powder and hastily preparing sacrifices to ward off evil spirits. All were mourning. The patient was lying on a mat and an old woman, armed with a fragment of broken bottle, was leaning over her, making incisions in her side and in the soles of her feet. Capitaine Docteur thrust aside the witch and also another woman who wanted to massage the patient with oil reserved for a fetish.

"I'll see to her," he said curtly. "Doéllé, look after the child."

"Where's the baby?" I asked these tearful peasants.

"The baby?" cried the father. "Scoundrel—ruffian! It wanted to kill my wife, the blackguard!"

With a jerk of his chin he indicated a baby abandoned in the corner; the navel cord had been severed with a split reed, but no one had troubled to wash the infant and powder it with maize flour. My efforts to revive the tiny life were unhappily useless. Meanwhile the mother opened her eyes and looked with a dazed air at the commotion going on around her.

"She's saved," said Capitaine Docteur.

At once the peasants who had been so bitterly lamenting leaped about for joy, and the happy cry rang out repeatedly: "*Allé lé ô! Allé lé ô!*"

"You're very cheerful," said the doctor reproachfully, "and yet your child's dead."

"That's nothing!" answered the man, his face stretched in laughter. "A little water spilt. The pitcher's not broken."

We had spent two hours in that hut. What had been going on between Urgèle and Flavien while the doctor and I wrestled to snatch two creatures from death? I walked quickly back, impatient to see Flavien's face. But Madame Docteur was alone beneath the crudely modeled hand and heart. Yaya in a leisurely manner was laying plates on the folding table. The mason wasp was

113

still buzzing. Urgèle was reading on a long chair lent by the chief; she seemed sad and worried.

"Frantz," she said, "Flavien asked me to say good-by to you for him, with his apologies. He was in a great hurry and couldn't wait until you came back."

7

*Kasli be nusianuke so aghato b'alo
me nyo ne dudu eda so ego me do bu
edu agheto b'alo so e wu.*

(Said the monkey: All that comes from
the hand of man is good to eat. But the
serpent, misunderstanding, bit the man's
hand and killed him.)

GONE was my proud assurance.

In Manoho, passion began darting and flickering over
the ground like wildfire. It attacked Urgèle the more
violently because she still desperately sought to flee from
it; it scorched Flavien in the courthouse; it licked the
heels of Capitaine Docteur and seemed ready to leap up
at him and at all the white people of the station. The
harmattan was coming.

On my return the sour lagoon, bound in its ring of

sickly palms, gave me a sign: "Didn't I warn you? I told you that other days would come. . . . They're coming. I foretell only truth, and truth is like soap—it never rots."

Ill-temperedly I shrugged my shoulders, turned my back and slipped on a white overall, and asked to see the register of births. Work would prevent my thinking: "What must I do? My thoughts have not been strong enough to part Urgèle and Flavien. Must I appeal to the witch? Or shall I try my luck once more by going to see Flavien tonight? I don't know. Quiet, now—that's enough. I'll think about it later."

"Amavi, the miscarriage hut has not been swept for three days at least—it's a disgrace. I shall report it to Capitaine Docteur and you'll be reprimanded. And you've been allowing that mother to eat *gombo*—are you mad? Do you want to kill her baby? Every time I leave you alone on duty something goes wrong."

Amazed at my harsh tone the second nurse hung her head. It did me good to lose my temper with a defenseless person.

Life went on. Madame Docteur barely spoke to me; we said good morning to one another and that was all. I no longer went to her bungalow at every odd moment, to supervise the making of a pineapple tart or to press a tulle frock. But from a distance I watched her lose day by day her look of unreality. She didn't walk now as if she were dancing—she didn't look like a seagull— she was just a joyless woman.

In the colonies there can be no happiness for a white

woman who loves outside her marriage. It's true that she saw Flavien every evening, but always at some gathering in the D.O.'s bungalow or at the cassava planter's. They were never alone for an instant. Sometimes the chances of an excursion found them in the same car. Then at last they were able to talk, and I imagined the jerky, broken phrases: "Do you love me, Urgèle? Why did you dance three times with the D.O. last night? You must dance only with me, d'you hear?"—"That's impossible. What about Doéllé, do you still see her?"—"Well, it's like this: I can't snub her. I must"—"I loathe you"—"And I detest you for having a husband who never leaves you for a moment"—"It's not the same thing"—"It's a thousand times worse"—"It's not!" They relapsed perhaps into angry silence, spoiling the unhoped-for moment of solitude. A kiss would have resolved the discord, but in front of their vehicle was the doctor's truck, and behind came the schoolmaster in his car. They were held prisoners between the tail lamp of the one and the headlights of the other. Almost at once they would have to separate, join in general conversation, and pretend to laugh; because of course these parties are supposed to be great fun. Misunderstandings piled up between Urgèle and Flavien, while keen, envious, or malevolent glances pierced them through. And the moon was shining—a lovers' moon. It was torment to see the moon shine for everyone instead of for themselves alone; and it went on shining, shining on the sea.

A quick pressure of the hands in passing a book—a touch of the knee under the cloth—the spurious embrace of a tango—these were all that the tropics allowed them; and soon these daily meetings were more painful than absence, more to be dreaded than separation.

"I daren't go out with you," Madame Docteur would no doubt murmur, "but Frantz will soon be off on another bush trek. I shan't go with him; you can come and see me and we'll talk."

The magistrate smiled his bitter, half-skeptical smile. Nevertheless the day came at last when the doctor left. Several cases of smallpox had been reported in the Lumé direction, where an old woman was said to have been robbed of six yards of cloth and in her fury had invoked the smallpox. Despite vaccination, symptoms of the disease had appeared on some of the inhabitants.

Kankwe brought me scraps of conversation he had picked up while waiting at table.

"Wait for me here a few days," Capitaine Docteur had said to his wife. "You can read and rest yourself, and call on Elisabeth or the planter's wife. Time will pass quickly, you'll see! I'm only sorry that there's this coldness between you and Doéllé since our last trip; she could have kept you company while I'm away and you'd have felt less lonely."

"Is it quite impossible for you to take me with you?"

"Quite. It wouldn't be at all wise."

Urgèle bowed her head in submission to the destiny that so well served her secret desire.

Hardly had the medical truck left on its journey to Lumé when I saw Madame Docteur going down to the hospital to telephone. I was in the maternity clinic busy scrubbing my hands, and I smiled because the magistrate, unaware of this sudden departure, was away at an inquest in the bush. This would be a keen disappointment to Urgèle, who expected him to come running at once. And indeed it was with a dispirited air that she climbed the steps again, her hands hanging limply at her sides against the green frock. "I never have any luck," she must have been thinking. "Here I am alone, as good as free, and Flavien's away. Will he get back before Frantz, even?"

Under the raised *sekos* I watched her all that day, wandering about the house like a troubled soul and counting minute by minute the wasted hours, the lost delight. Amalia the mulatto sat sewing, indifferent and silent, looking at the lagoon and sighing. The Child of the Moon, crouched over his short broom, swept the floors. Madame Docteur was alone. The palm trees near the hospital swayed listlessly, the nursing orderlies moved about with the fewest possible gestures and words, and pirogues hollowed a sluggish wake through the water. Would it rain at last? Every moment or so someone raised his head, fancying he had felt a drop. But no.

Leaning on her elbows like Amalia the mulatto, Madame Docteur also was scanning the clouds. Above all she scanned the road. But beside it there stood only the great baobab, the one that donned a white blanket at night and went about choosing its dead; and upon the road nothing but the slow coming and going of natives hoping for rain.

One last truck set down at the hospital entrance a family of *évolués* carrying thermos bottles, green socks, guitars, and pink chamberpots. And in one moment the gray, livid pallor of the sky melted into blackness.

Madame Docteur lit the lamp. How unutterably alone she felt! The boys, silent for once, were nowhere to be seen. She lay down on the bed that was covered with a Sudanese cotton counterpane, and tried to read. A sticky wind swelled the curtains slightly as on other evenings, the waters boomed along the bar regularly and inexorably. Sometimes a dull thud made her start: an overripe banana had dropped from the bunch hanging in the veranda, peeling itself as it did so, to lie stripped and squashy on the floor where it was immediately attacked by long black streams of ants.

She left her room and for some time wandered about the dead house, among the cowrie-hung helmets, rusty assagais, and stiff panther hides that were awaiting the tanner. Parcels of green coffee beans done up in sacking were stacked on the desk ready for dispatch to friends at home; nothing remained but to write the addresses on the labels. Yet day after day Madame Docteur postponed this petty task. For a moment she looked at these parcels with their blank labels, then turned to switch on the radio. With great difficulty she found Brazzaville which, with confused squeaks and chirpings and abrupt breaks, was giving a program of songs.

"Edith Piaf . . . *Les amants de Paris ont de drôles de*

*chansons, les amants de Paris ont de drôles de façons . . .
Il y a des gens bizarres . . . Il sentait bon le sable
chaud . . ."*

Enough of that. When one's far away and alone, the
wireless that at first brings a sense of home and security
soon makes one feel even more remote and lonely. The
distance between two continents thus linked stretches
out interminably. Madame Docteur soon began to long
for the boys' return; when she had switched off the radio
she yearned for the sound of their cackling, which as a
rule maddened her. Perhaps she would have welcomed
even my own appearance on the doorstep, as in former
days. She would endure anything to escape from the
silence, the dread, the crushing weight of this loneliness
—to be able to talk to someone, no matter whom.

At the time when we were still friends she said one
day, "Life here is a burden because one can never talk.
I mean really talk—talk about oneself. Smiles, polite-
ness, arguments, cocktails—yes; but people are all on
their guard and never show themselves as they really are.
In Paris I had an old servant—she was like a mother to
me. I could talk to her about myself for hours on end
and she'd listen without ever seeming bored. When I
repeated myself she pretended not to notice it. But these
people don't listen, they are thinking of their own affairs
and following their own train of thought, even if they
seem to be interested in what you're saying. If you really
want to see them happy and at ease you must talk about
them, always and everlastingly."

She was so touching and vulnerable, with her pathetic

voice, that I wanted to say to her: "I could listen to you —I could listen as patiently as your old servant, but you wouldn't have to pay me to do it. Talk as much as you like about yourself, Madame Docteur, and repeat over and over again whatever pleases you. I'll listen."

But that time had passed. Madame Docteur looked at me with hostility when we met. I didn't have to listen to her any more; and she, quite alone in the night, had no one to talk to.

Next day, an orderly told me, Flavien rang her up. He must have heard of the doctor's departure—everything becomes known here, and swiftly—and hurried back to Manoho, having rushed the inquest. At siesta time he drew up, affectedly casual, opposite the hospital.

The boys were sniggering already as they prepared to peer and listen and report to me. Thanks to their shameless vigilance I learned all that Flavien and Urgèle did and said.

"I was over near Agouké," said the magistrate in an unnatural voice. "It was a complicated business with endless palavering. As usual. A man whose father had died inherited from two wives. He was supposed to allow his younger brother three pounds sterling in compensation, but he couldn't pay. In his shame he committed suicide with some ant-killer containing arsenic."

She gazed at him intently, revealing in her eyes all yesterday's waiting and loneliness and fear. Flavien without another word drew behind the frame of a shutter on the veranda and took her in his arms.

He covered her neck with kisses, and her cheeks and lips, while Urgèle leaned against his shoulder as on that day in the cemetery; she let herself droop there with that sad surrender that made one long to protect her. But they were not to be left long in peace. I had paid the boys to prowl about them on one pretext or another, and now Kankwe came to ask for the key of the store cupboard. "Madame, the cat wants some rice." Then I sent along an old woman I knew, who offered to massage Urgèle with butter.

"Not now; I'm busy. Perhaps later," said Madame Docteur in a tone of annoyance. She sat down on the little divan and Flavien took the rattan chair opposite, like any commonplace caller.

"We can't put up with this any longer, Urgèle," he said sternly.

Just then someone clapped at the foot of the steps; it was Madame Elisabeth. Her daughter was with her, carrying a doll slung on her back as usual.

"I hope I'm not disturbing you?" she said, with a treacherous smile directed at the magistrate. "Dear Madame, I heard you were alone, so I came to say good morning and to ask you to dine with us tonight. Here are a few fashion papers which I thought might pass the time while your husband is away."

She sat down beside Urgèle and began turning the pages of the magazines she had brought, talking meanwhile of flutings, flounces, pleated skirts and necklines, and asking about the latest Paris dress shows. She was delighted to have burst into this tête-à-tête and reveled in ruining it by her chatter. The patches on her ankles and wrists seemed whiter than ever, but she had taken up a becoming pose that revealed the suppleness of her body. She sought to catch Flavien's eye, but Flavien smoked and looked down his nose, enveloped in chill solitude, resolutely silent.

"This weather's very trying, isn't it?" went on Madame Elisabeth, tightening her belt. "Soon we shall all be gasping for rain. Rain! I can't say the word without thinking of when Adeline was born. We were at Djougou then, in Dahomey. The river had overflowed and the roads had been blocked by a tornado. The doctor couldn't reach us, so my husband got through to him on the telephone and managed the whole thing himself, following the instructions of the doctor from minute to minute—almost from second to second—at the end of the line . . ."

As if impelled by a spring the magistrate leaped up from the rattan chair.

"I must get back to the courthouse," he said rudely. "I'd forgotten an appointment with a chief."

He bowed to the two women abruptly and left; I heard the purr of his engine fading in the distance. But the boys, seeing Flavien beat a retreat, burst into shameless laughter. They laughed till they choked, loudly and shrilly. Madame Docteur interrupted her visitor, who was now talking of feeding bottles and diapers, and addressed them harshly:

"Well, what's the matter? Why all this noise? What or whom are you laughing at?"

"Nothing, Madame," Yaya assured her. "Not you. We're just talking." But there was still a gleam in his eyes.

It was defeat, another defeat for Urgèle and Flavien. I was sure that henceforth Madame Docteur would not venture to receive sentimental visits in the absence of her husband, and was therefore surprised to see Flavien returning the following evening at six o'clock.

"I thought perhaps you might let me come and fetch you," he said very loudly, so that the boys might hear him. "I've arranged for a pirogue to be ready; I want to show you the other lagoon and the alligators."

"But I'm terrified of alligators—almost as frightened as I am of pythons!"

"These are musical-comedy ones. The natives say they've made a pact with men. 'No guns,' said the men. 'No man-eating,' said the alligators. And everyone lives at peace in the lagoon. There's nothing to be afraid of. You may get a chance to see a criminal, ostracized by his fellow alligators. My boy Amedéwovoé assures me it happens sometimes."

"Oh, I'd hate to miss that! Very well, I'll come."

The light, almost gay tone they affected was for the benefit of Bokari, who was cleaning a mat at the end of the veranda. Their pitiful act was staged for Amalia the mulatto who, supremely indifferent, was finishing the hemming of a sheet. Madame Docteur took up her sun helmet and strove to walk calmly toward Flavien's car, restraining as best she might her impulse to run and skip.

Alas, I cannot tell what they said to one another in the pirogue. Certainly Flavien could never have kissed her, for the second lagoon was bordered by a road frequented by natives. The brief twilight splashed sky and water with a vivid pink, while along the green shores countless birds moved about on swift, slender legs: herons, egrets, and flamingoes daubed with pink like the sky and the water.

Nor do I know whether they found a criminal among the alligators. But on her return at seven o'clock Madame Docteur ran up the steps with a gay liveliness that I had never seen in her before.

Next day, on the pretext of buying fish, they went out again. A narrow beach twenty-five miles long links Manoho with Tocono, and the couple fancied perhaps that they would be as indistinguishable on this expanse as two grains of sand. But fishermen noted the car parked under a coconut palm, and children set off in search of the white people, laughing and joking in advance. Urgèle and Flavien looked very small sitting there by the sea, so the children told me. The salt dampness must have soaked their clothes and the sand stuck to their legs and hands. A ship with all her lights on appeared over the horizon and I can imagine that Flavien and Urgèle, confronted with this image of forbidden freedom, knew the despair of castaways.

They would have gone out together again, I'm sure, if the doctor had not sent word of his return next day. Ah, thank God! I heaved a sigh of relief at this news, which greeted me on my return from Waji. I had spent the day with my family for the baptism of my brother Foli's son. Océa and I had brought the ritual presents for the eighth day: a basin, a brush, a mosquito net, a lantern, and a can of kerosene. The baby was brought out and it was my task to throw a calabashful of water up onto the thatch, so that it fell back onto the child's body. "Let's hope," said I, "that one day he'll have true Christian baptism." But they all burst out laughing, and Océa according to custom began cutting the baby's nails and hair. Leaving Amérique to drink palm wine with the guests I went back to the maternity clinic just in time to learn of Capitaine Docteur's return.

The night was growing deeper. A Hausa woman had been brought in while I was away, with a dead child in her womb. Eclampsia occurs fairly often in our country. The African doctor had bled her, the midwives had delivered her and it was for me to tend her now. Like most patients she had refused to lie on the fiber mattress and remained stretched upon her mat on the ground, quite motionless. A relation of hers had already bound her turban about her head: a blue turban with white stripes that was complex and beautiful and ennobled her face. I prepared to watch beside her all night.

A lamp was burning in Madame Docteur's room a

few steps away. I imagined Urgèle shut within the folds of her mosquito net as within a cage; wherever she might be, whether on the alligator lagoon, by the sea, or in bed she was always a prisoner. I could feel that she was half smothered and bathed in sweat. Her foot sought vainly for a bit of dry sheet. When she turned she swam in sticky moisture and her soaked hair trailed over her cheeks; she looked like one drowned. And despite the infusion of citronella that she had drunk after dinner she was not asleep—she could not sleep: Capitaine Docteur was coming back next day.

It was the hour when cockroaches and black beetles take possession of kitchens and showers, and white ants are busy mining in the woodwork. Outside, animals prowled, swishing through the undergrowth. A fowl seized by a tiger cat uttered a shriek of agony, answered by the squeals of the newborn baby in Hut Three. Madame Docteur heard these two cries as I did, and as clearly; the maternity clinic was separated from her bungalow by only a little red sand and a few coconut palms. If I'd troubled to listen I could have heard her breathe.

"How shall we live without our walks together?" she must have been wondering. "Will Frantz discover that I've seen Flavien three times while he was away? What will he say? I know him so little—I never know how he'll react."

Everyone in Manoho knew of her guilty love. The D.O. who came to see her one morning, bringing a native carving of a three-headed bird, did not conceal from her his chagrin at being supplanted by the magistrate. This afternoon the planter's wife came to fetch Urgèle in her car to take her to Tocono; a messageries boat lay at the wharf and all the white women wanted to go aboard and buy a scarf or some scent from France, and to breathe, in the air-conditioned bar, a little of its atmosphere. "Thank you, Madame," Urgèle had said, "it's very kind of you but I'm afraid I'm engaged this afternoon." The one-time nun showed her disapproval by a pinched smile and went alone to Tocono, where she confided to all her acquaintances that the flighty Madame Docteur was about to make a fool of her admirable husband, if she hadn't already done so.

The infant in Hut Three went on yelling. Its cries maddened me, though I was well used to the noise. The Hausa woman with the complicated turban stared at me from her mat without moving, without speaking. There was now no look of illness about her; she appeared quite well. I felt her pulse: it was regular. Her temperature was normal. She had turned the corner evidently, and didn't need me. I would go and wake Amavi and she would look in on her now and again. Then I would take Flavien by surprise; I would talk to him and try to convince him.

Passing in front of Urgèle's bungalow I was all defiance. I'm not beaten yet, Madame Docteur. We shall see who wins. Poor Urgèle behind her mosquito net with her tormenting thoughts! But I was going to Flavien . . .

In the middle of the lagoon fishermen were tapping on their pirogue to attract the fish. I left the monotonous sound behind me, and the roll of the surf on the bar. Round the courthouse flying foxes uttered their sharp cries, and I reflected that it was because of these that Flavien hated to be alone. He said their squeaking drove him mad, especially when he had a bout of malaria. And he had one that night. I could see it at once from his feverish eyes, the burning cigarette in the ash tray near his bed, and the glass of whisky standing untouched. The room was lit only by the moon—a moon almost as bright as the sun. Flavien watched me come in without a word, and never moved even when I began to undress. He was too tired to say no.

Would he stop me getting into bed? No. His teeth were chattering, he was chilled to the bone, and powerless to argue. Stretched out motionless on the edge of the mattress I waited. He lay as still as myself and bit the sheet to stifle the rattle of his teeth.

"Will he soon fall asleep?" I wondered, silent as a statue. "Who knows—perhaps he'll let something slip then and dream aloud. And I shall learn things—things I don't know."

Time passed and the flying foxes had been crying for some time when he fell asleep. Instinctively he drew nearer to me and even rested his head on my shoulder. I was made happy by this fleeting joy; a slight joy indeed. If he came back to me, I told myself, I wouldn't reproach him; I would be gentle and kind. I dared not stroke his cropped head for fear of waking him. But he opened his eyes suddenly and when he saw me so close to him he swore. He drew away, cursing me, malaria, and flying foxes; he rolled himself violently in the sheet and turned over to the extreme edge of the bed. Even in his sleep he was resolved to remain faithful to Madame Docteur.

About the courthouse the night quivered, panted, suffered, screeched, hunted, and loved. I stayed open-eyed and watchful. Flavien was fretting himself to pieces because I wasn't Urgèle; between the sheets that he threw off in his fever Urgèle would have been so lovely. But he, a pariah, had no right to more than vain excursions on the lagoon, along the roads or on the beach. Never, never would he hold Madame Docteur naked in his bed—naked, as I was. Never would he know the whole sweetness of her body—nothing but a stolen touch, hasty, furtive, and unfulfilled.

Soon he began to hate me silently for being there beside him, so naked, so offered. I followed his thought: Urgèle beside him, relaxed and at peace—Urgèle's fair hair on his scarred shoulder. . . .

When now and then he turned abruptly and lay face downward it was to crush his uncontrolled desire for her. He dived down into the mattress to defend himself against my detested attack. I wanted him so much that night; and he so longed for Urgèle. Two people, one white and one black, each at the edge of the bed with their lonely desire.

From the direction of Waji came the melancholy sound of a drum. One beat. A long silence. Then three.

A silence. One beat. Silence. Three beats. Silence. One beat. I knew it was the funeral drum for one of my distant cousins. He had died in Accra, but at Waji they were ceremonially interring his nails and hair brought with all speed by a messenger. Flavien, maddened by the monotonous and sinister throbs, heaved a great sigh— and this human sigh hid for a moment the love cries of the flying foxes. I would have liked to stroke the cropped head and say very softly: "I understand. . . . I'm sorry for you. I'll be patient and humble. I'll wait. . . . I'll wait as long as you like."

But I dared not touch his electrified skin, his flayed skin. He would have struck me, perhaps even killed me.

Burning with fever he rose at last and paced the terrace, his hands in the pockets of his pajamas. He was recollecting that tomorrow night at this time Capitaine Docteur would be peacefully sleeping beside Urgèle— and it was intolerable to think of Urgèle beside anyone but himself. From Waji the drum pulsed on: one beat, pause, three beats, pause, one beat. . . .

I lay as if lifeless. Flattened like an animal who feels the approach of a tornado I waited for the moment when he would throw me off the bed, roaring, "I've had enough. Get out and never come back!"

But he said not a word and, soothed by the coolness that attends the ending of night, he lay down again. At first cockcrow he fell into a troubled sleep; I leaned on my elbow and watched him. He lay close to me, yet how unattainable! And at this thought I felt a pain at my heart. Formerly, sentiment left but a fleeting impression on me, but the white company I had so imprudently kept had introduced me to a world of passions I should never otherwise have suspected. What at first had been humiliation and stung pride became keen suffering. I discovered that love is not merely a pleasure and a natural source of joy, but also a well of grief.

Day had risen. In all the neighboring huts women were fastening their blankets and sweeping, according to custom, before their husbands awoke. Amedéwovoé, Flavien's boy, stretched himself yawning in front of the courthouse.

"*Eso bedo*, Doéllé. You seem sad this morning. Look, I'll cheer you up with a riddle. Tell me what this is: *ho dele ho deme*—a hut within a hut?"

"I don't know. I hate riddles, Amedéwovoé."

"A hut within a hut is a mosquito net. Well, go on— laugh! Why don't you laugh? Here's another riddle for you. Ha, ha! *Yiyi mea, mi zo gazome, gbogbo mea mi zo tenu tenu.* Going it hangs, coming it stands. What is it, Doéllé?" He grimaced obscenely toward the courthouse, his eyes and teeth all laughter.

"Let me pass, Amedéwovoé. Your riddles are very silly this morning."

"Going it hangs, coming it stands. It's a water pitcher, Doéllé, that's all! Just a water pitcher on a woman's head."

He was still laughing when I entered the cemetery on the way to the maternity clinic—"Just a water pitcher, Doéllé!"

I began running. My heart hurt again as it had during

133

the night. White people are always ready to cry, "My heart is broken!" At last I knew what they meant. My heart was broken into little bits that were bleeding inside my breast.

At the maternity clinic Amavi told me that the Hausa woman had just died. Her blue turban, so complex and so beautiful, had not shifted on her forehead by a millimeter.

8

Ame jiro viku lolo mu kpo na enu wu
ahue to wo.

(The wide-eyed stranger sees no more
than the owner of the house.)

CAPITAINE DOCTEUR had been dining at the
courthouse. Amedéwovoé served coffee on the little terrace and listened to the conversation.

"I'm thinking of taking Urgèle on my next trip to the
north. She's interested in the leper villages. Why not
come with us, Flavien?"

Capitaine Docteur threw out the question carelessly,
while lighting his pipe. But the muscle in his jaw quivered a little; the quiver was beyond his control, as were
his flushes and pallors and the occasional tapping of his
fingers.

135

"You know I can't come," said Flavien cautiously. "There are the court sittings, evidence to be collected out in the bush—judicial business of all kinds keeps me a prisoner here, unfortunately."

"You could easily get a fortnight's leave. You need it too, I think; you look tired. Go on, come with us!"

"I'll think about it. Thanks for asking me."

Flavien was torn between the desire of being with Madame Docteur and the torment of knowing that he would never be alone with her during the trek. Which way should he decide? His eyes sought those of Urgèle, and her slowly lowered lashes answered, "Come!"

Thus it was that the three of them set óff northward to meet the harmattan.

I still wonder what impelled Capitaine Docteur to take Flavien as traveling companion. Until then he had not shown any particular interest in him. Indeed, outside his work the doctor paid little heed to anyone; he never volunteered his friendship or confided in others. Madame Elisabeth, whom he was treating just now for an abscess on the neck, must have adroitly aroused some uneasiness in his mind, warned him against Flavien, perhaps, or insinuating that Urgèle had altered. "Oh, very little, of course, but still—" Being a methodical man he may have wanted to gain evidence of the truth or falsehood of these tales by remaining at close quarters with his wife and Flavien for a fortnight. In his place I should never have tried to verify anything; I should have removed Urgèle very promptly to a great distance. He summoned danger; he went to meet it. Did he hope that the daily constraint of their meeting would weary the culprits, exasperate and wear them down until it finally parted them? I don't know—I don't know.

But when I saw their cars loaded with boys and equipment disappearing in a cloud of red dust I was filled with a great distress. I had not seen Flavien since that night in the courthouse, but at least I had known he was there, breathing the same air, and I could sense his presence. Suddenly he had escaped; I could not watch the progress of his love.

So *this* was parting: this ever-deepening emptiness—this hunger and thirst that no food or drink could satisfy. Sometimes in the beginning I thought I was really hungry and thirsty, and I hastened to eat some *akaassa* or a little *gombo* and to drink a glass of palm wine, believing that I should then feel better. But, alas, my hunger and my burning thirst remained.

It is said in these parts that the soul easily escapes from its fleshy covering, to perch at the top of a teak or a baobab. Soon my own anguished soul left my body and acquired the habit of sitting at the top of the sacred baobab. My soul turned its back on Capitaine Docteur's deserted bungalow and gazed into the far, far distance —to the roads of the north.

The landscape looked blurred and vague, and the horizon quivered. Where they were the bush was ablaze; their truck was moving between two walls of fire at top speed, lest the gasoline vapor should catch alight. The suffocating heat of sun and fire combined dried the throat and stung the eyes with scattered ash. Flames,

137

scarcely visible in the blinding sunlight, delicately brushed the floor of the clearings—delicately, like frisking goats, so that one wanted to play with them. Then suddenly they plunged into the thickets, hurled themselves furiously at the trees in sudden jets, in curtains, in walls. Even from here in Manoho, where the lagoon sparkled in the silence, I seemed to hear the silky rending of lianas. I had often traveled in the north in the season of bush fires, and I could imagine how the khayas repelled the assault with the impassivity of fortresses, while other trees spouted sap from every branch. As we say here: "The wide-eyed stranger sees no better than the owner of the house." I know those districts well. I had seen hardwoods panting and staggering, while dull explosions punctuated the resinous bubbling of acacias.

It occurred to me that Flavien and Urgèle could have found no setting to reflect their passion so fiercely as did this. Life held in a stranglehold by death—savagely as a deer shot in mid leap—that is hell. A hell of the senses to scorch the very blood.

In that fire began their triple existence, their agonizing intimacy.

Every evening, weary, with parched skins and hoarse voices, they halted at a resthouse: an inn without sheets or sign. There was no ceiling; the thatched roof on its rafters of fan palm that is proof against rot, suspended over the travelers its thick, uneven cords. Yaya brought water to the dusty shower and put into use an old German filter of white porcelain, while Kankwe roasted a guinea fowl shot during the day. Urgèle changed her shorts and began to open baskets and bring out bottles of wine wrapped in damp cloths. Intimacy: Urgèle's toothbrush beside Flavien's, Capitaine Docteur's dressing gown over that of the magistrate. One evening Amedéwovoé, by the light of the hurricane lamp, removes a jigger from the sole of Flavien's foot. He dislodges the little ball of eggs with an orange stick, but it's Urgèle who brings the mercurochrome and dabs it on the wound.

Again, under the apparently indifferent gaze of Capitaine Docteur, Flavien squeezes green lemons and measures out the rum for Urgèle's drink. Flavien sees Urgèle every moment of the day; he guesses when she's hungry, knows the slight tensing of her lips when she's sleepy, and the smell of her sweat. She is not afraid to appear before him with ruffled hair, unmade-up and sometimes plain; she's aware of being thus more moving and desirable. Urgèle lives as near him as if she were his wife, but he may not touch her. He can only clench behind him his hard, useless hands.

One evening by tacit consent they stayed up later than usual, drinking and smoking in the compound, watching the flicker of distant bush fires and filling the silence with desultory remarks. Still, one must go to bed sometime! As a rule their beds are made up in the same room, Urgèle's beside her husband's, while somewhat apart Flavien's luminous watch sweeps the darkness; for he makes wide, restless movements. In turning Urgèle causes her bed to creak slightly and Flavien wonders savagely why the bed creaks thus. . . . The night grows pale. A baboon barks among the rocks, or else it's the farewell cry of an antelope caught by some beast of prey. And always, always through the cracks in the wall comes the chattering of geckoes. Urgèle and Flavien, a few inches apart, await the first cockcrow to relax a little; the first light of day that allows words, for lack of caresses, to be exchanged through the mosquito netting.

I gathered some of these details from the boys, Kankwe, Yaya, and Amedéwovoé, but the underlying emotional mood I learned by other means. My friend Amérique knew a young virgin in Waji of the name of Jabellé who had the gift of second sight, and to please me he summoned her several times to his hut. He had crushed the shell of the insect called *temigougou* and the leaves of the *ablakan*, a crawling plant containing a vegetable fluid of powerful magnetism. The resulting powder he set before the girl in seven little heaps; Jabellé bent over them and inhaled from each in turn. Soon her eyes rolled upward and in unison with us she murmured the ritual phrase: "*Arijanio neva!* Let the spirits come! *Arijanio neva!*" Then she fell asleep. I had but to question her and she answered with eyes closed; she mimicked the scenes she described without knowing the actors, throwing her head back like Urgèle, drumming her fingers nervously like Capitaine Docteur, impressing on her young, black, sweating face all Flavien's bitterness.

In this way I learned many things.

"I can't stand any more. Let's go back to Manoho!"

140

Madame Docteur would plead, after those sleepless nights filled with the chattering of geckoes.

"We're going on," Capitaine Docteur replied quietly, without even looking at her.

And they set off once more. I imagined the earth blackened, stripped, charred, and desolate, as I myself had seen it on my journey through the north. Here and there baobabs stood up like huge whitened bones. Sometimes the white people's eyes rested, momentarily refreshed, on the sudden defiant green of an acacia spared by the fire, or on the brilliant yellow of a cotton flower in a field of ashes. Living creatures now appeared before the car: they were naked and black and smeared with gray, and held themselves erect in the eddying heat, erect in the incandescence. They did not smile. These were lepers. Women pounded millet in wooden mortars, throwing heavy pestles into the air, clapping their hands, and catching them again. These too were lepers. Bluebottles clustered about their sores and their reddened eyes. From time to time a lovely young girl would pass, burden on head, and one thought: "Thank God she's not a leper!" Then one spied a shiny patch on her shoulder—a silvery gleam like that of an old scar.

The chief who received the white travelers wore a cap of monkey skin adorned with toucan feathers, magnificent indeed. But where his nose should have been there was nothing but a monstrous fungus. The village looked like any other village, with its thatched roofs pinched as it were into points, its babies rolling in the dust and its black pigs poking their snouts into the lopsided entries to the huts. But these men who so tranquilly cultivated their groundnuts, cotton, and pigeon peas had sometimes no fingers, toes, or ears.

Had she not been blinded by love, Madame Docteur would have shuddered to learn that healthy women lived here with their leprous husbands, fearless of contagion. But Urgèle was not worrying about lepers. Flavien was beside her; his shoulder hid the world from her. If she had been asked to live shut up forever in a leper village she would have consented so long as Flavien might be with her.

A week had passed since their departure from Manoho. Capitaine Docteur had not left them alone together for one instant; he was always there watching them, and the intensity of his pent-up emotion rendered his society unbearably oppressive.

"Give me one second alone with Flavien, I beg of you, Frantz!" was Urgèle's silent entreaty. "I must speak to him for a second—no more than a second. Go and talk to the African orderlies, supervise the chaulmoogra-oil injections, go to the sleeping-sickness clinic —do anything, only leave me alone for one instant with Flavien! Have you no pity?"

But Capitaine Docteur insisted that Urgèle should go with him to meet his colleague at the sleeping-sickness hospital; that she should look on at the chaulmoogra-oil injections and be beside him when he questioned the nurses. Then she would say wearily, "You planned this trip for me, didn't you? It was to be a sort of holiday.

Don't make a forced march of it. Let's go back to Manoho, Frantz!"

And Capitaine Docteur, calm and inflexible, replied, "We have another week. We'll go on."

And Urgèle and Flavien went on, like victims whom Capitaine Docteur was dissecting with the scalpel of his jealousy.

9

Ehù l'ado me too wo tu na tâ gé.

(Blood is in the stomach, yet one spits
white.)

MOUNTAINS had closed in behind the car and the
three Europeans were driving among huge, parched
fields of millet. Soon the fortresses appeared: orange-
colored, crenelated, flanked by three turrets that were
the granaries. Little lost worlds—wild places where men
kill each other for a handful of grain and where the
smallest argument whips the poisoned arrow from the
quiver.

"I thought this wild country might interest you, Urgèle," said Capitaine Docteur. "The chatelaines of these
strange castles go naked but for a string between the
legs, while the men wear only a hollowed gourd."

144

But Urgèle took about as much interest in the naked men as she did in the lepers. Silently she drove her sharp nails into Flavien's arm—he was now at the wheel—drove them into his flesh like a maddened panther to show him beyond all doubt that nothing interested her but him. Beside her, Capitaine Docteur observed her action; and he who for two years had hidden all his feelings and feigned indifference in all circumstances, now seized Urgèle by the shoulder and drew her to himself with a rough, possessive movement.

Madame Docteur lay rigid in this unexpected grasp, but soon freed herself.

"Forgive me, Frantz, but it's so terribly hot."

She shook back her hair and dabbed her forehead with a little green handkerchief. Flavien went on driving, pretending to have noticed neither Urgèle's claws nor the doctor's movement. He drove easily and naturally with only two slight swerves into the edge of the millet—swerves which the boys afterward told me of and which my imagination seized upon at once.

No one spoke. This journey, begun in a sort of exaltation and uncertainty, was to end in silence: a silence growing day by day more sultry.

Beneath the fine lacy leaves and the purple pompoms of the *nérés* the camping place came into sight. A guard advanced to meet the white people, swinging his hippopotamus-hide whip; his khaki jacket was of regulation pattern, but from the waist downward he was stark naked. The chief came too, with a dagger fixed to his arm and the genitals bound and tied up against his belly with a cord. But the rest of the population, instead of running up inquisitively as in other villages, kept away with a sort of hostile indifference. The resthouse itself was ostentatiously bare: no shower, no windows, and no chairs, only seats roughly hollowed out of the wall. The boys began preparing the evening meal without enthusiasm: they felt ill at ease among these backward peoples who had neither clothes, schools, nor dispensaries and who considered the newcomers from the coast as contemptible foes.

Night fell on the red mud castles with their uneven crenelations. While the three whites in their hollowed-out seats ate in silence by the light of the hurricane lamp on the ground, men passed before the hut without turning their heads, silent also, with an iron stud in each nostril, an iron cone in the ear, and the sex organs uncovered or encased in a sheath.

Not even the cry of an animal was to be heard. Sometimes there came the flabby fall of a mango, and indeed a whole carpet of rotting fruit covered the ground as far as the boys' quarters.

Unable to endure the tense, exacerbating atmosphere Flavien rose and without a word of apology went outside. And while with relief he breathed the free air, the nervous strain under which Urgèle had labored for so many days broke at last.

"Oh, Frantz," she cried, in a voice quivering with unshed tears, "this is unbearable. This was to have been a treat for me and you've turned it into something horrible. Why do you punish me so? It's as if you wanted to take some sort of revenge. Why? The very air around us is poisoned."

Urgèle had sprung from her hollowed chair and was moving now around the hurricane lamp, so that her shadow, fantastically enlarged and deformed, swept over the walls of the hut, escaped as far as the rotten mangoes and joined the trunks of the *nérés*. Capitaine Docteur rose in his turn and with slow steps followed the distracted movements of Urgèle around the storm lantern on the ground.

"Please, Frantz, say something! Scold me, hit me if you like, but say something! I can't bear any more of this—I can't bear it!"

He still did not answer, but his eyes were hard as flint and a smile twitched at his lower lip. The boys, who missed nothing of this scene, assured me that their huge, twisted shadows were terrifying in the silence that was broken only by the pathetic voice of Urgèle.

"I've always been unhappy and lonely with you. You've never bothered to think what I might be feeling —you've never even tried to understand me, from the very beginning of our married life. You're nothing but a brutal egoist, incapable of—"

And with the dishonesty of erring wives Madame Docteur heaped reproaches on her husband, raked up old quarrels, bewailed her fate, and burst into tears.

"Stop whirling round the lamp like a mad thing," said Capitaine Docteur suddenly in an icy voice. "You look like a ham actress playing tragedy. Take two cachets of *gardénal* and go to sleep; that's the best thing you can do just now."

It was then that Flavien re-entered the hut. He had evidently heard everything. Without a word he lay down beneath his mosquito net at the far end of the room. Biting on the rolled-up ball of her handkerchief Urgèle lay down on the other bed. The lamp remained on the floor. Another mango joined the rotten mass upon the ground outside.

Capitaine Docteur had left the hut. Half an hour went by. The two lay imprisoned in their narrow mosquito nets, not daring to speak; they lay watchful, awaiting the return of this strange husband. An hour passed and still the doctor didn't come back. It was then that Urgèle grew frightened. She pictured the ferocious expression of those warriors with the iron-studded noses— the warriors who, as Flavien had assured her, were so quick to snatch the poisoned arrow from the quiver. Frantz was perhaps lying transfixed among the teak trees. Or suppose a panther had sprung suddenly from a thicket and hurled him to the ground? Frantz never walked about at night; if he had to go out he always took a lamp with him to light the path because of snakes. . . . For there were snakes too! Urgèle had forgotten that possibility. Suicide? But only unhinged, neurotic people made away with themselves. Frantz was balance and good sense itself. . . . Or was he? Might not his coldness be a mask to hide grief, shyness, everlastingly curbed impulses? Madame Docteur had never realized

148

before how very little she knew of this man who was her husband.

"I ought to have taken more interest in him. I ought to have asked him things—made him open up to me," she thought remorsefully. "All this is my fault."

She dressed again hurriedly and went to raise Flavien's mosquito net.

"Come with me," she ordered him. "We must go and see what's happened. Wake Amedéwovoé and we'll take torches and go and look for Frantz."

"Please, Urgèle, don't let's be in such a hurry. Better wait—he's sure to come back soon. Don't let's make bigger fools of ourselves than we need in front of the boys."

Madame Docteur fixed a wild eye on the magistrate.

"Of course! You don't think of my anxiety. If anything happened to Frantz you'd be more pleased than sorry, wouldn't you?"

"Urgèle, you're out of your mind!"

"Quite so, I'm crazy. And yet I've lived for years without all these shocks and explosions and scenes. It's true I was often bored, but at any rate I never went through such torture. Of all that I loved before I met you, nothing's left. Now I live in a desert of ashes, as if I'd been burned up in one of these forest fires. What have you brought me but trouble—and perhaps despair?"

"Urgèle, Urgèle! Can you really mean what you say?"

"I'm sorry, Flavien. I'm terrified and my words run

149

ahead of my thoughts. You see, if anything happened to Frantz there'd be nothing for me to do but kill myself."

Theatrical words in the night. These two forgot to address one another as 'thou' or to speak their love. For a few moments they must have loathed one another.

Taking Amedéwovoé with them they set off at random, swinging the hurricane lamp, in an absurd little procession heralded by the hoarse voice of Urgèle: "Frantz, Frantz, where are you?"

From time to time Flavien raised the lantern and gazed into the dense darkness. Silence alone replied.

"I'm frightened, Flavien—I'm frightened! Can these sacred serpents really revenge themselves? You know, at Christmas Frantz had to kill a python that was starting to strangle me. Does that dead python possess the power to follow him even here?"

"But Urgèle, that's simply a native myth! Don't tell me you believe such things. Please, please calm yourself. We shall find Frantz quite safe and sound—and probably in a foul temper. Believe me, he's not the sort to do away with himself or have accidents."

A short, bitter laugh escaped him. Then a red spark appeared before them, level with a field of yams—a little red spark that was the end of a cigarette. Frantz was walking steadily to meet this absurd expedition.

"Frantz! Where on earth have you been?"

Released from her fears, Madame Docteur allowed a note of anger to creep into her voice; she was now furious at having given way to superstition. Flavien had been right: Frantz was not the type to kill himself or have accidents. How stupid to have believed for a moment in the python's vengeance, and what a fool she had been to feel remorse and to behave so badly to Flavien.

"I just went for a walk," said the cold voice of Capitaine Docteur. "Haven't I even the right to do that?"

"You have every right to do anything," answered Urgèle in a trembling voice.

Frantz, Urgèle, and Flavien, followed by the sniggering Amedéwovoé, returned to the resthouse.

That evening, while the white people in the north were revolving excitedly around a storm lantern on the ground, I was eating cassava in my mother's house; for at this time I often went to Waji. At last I felt a little calmer. Flavien's absence, after the torments of those first days, was a relief and I breathed more freely. Also my mind was made up. The most trying and painful thing is indecision: wondering whether to take this line or that. Once the course of action is determined all is easier.

"Well, and does he still refuse to eat honey, Océa? When's the wedding?"

I joked with my sister as she was setting forth to meet her lover, her breasts shiny with cosmetics, her velvet robe bound low about her hips to set off the fine curve of the small of her back.

"In August. It'll be on a Thursday, to bring luck. In a few days Fossou will come and speak to Mother for the first time."

In this part of the world the betrothed must ask for a girl in marriage three times before being accepted.

"But what about you, Doéllé?" retorted Océa, showing her splendid teeth. "You're not so young now, and it's time for you to choose a husband. When is it to be? Never? Amérique's so fond of you, but he says you want to marry a white man."

"Amérique's crazy," I answered, laughing.

But I went to Amérique—crazy Amérique—in his hut and spent an hour or two with him. He was very congenial to me and I liked him more and more. While he slept I thought of our childhood together. I remembered how we went after mudfish, as they slept in pockets of mud after the rains. On dry land we caught crabs that were said to have slipped from the hands of *So*, the god of thunder. I remembered the days when my father consulted *Afan*, the oracle of the sixteen oil-palm nuts. I should have liked to share these memories with Amérique—to wake him gently and say, "Do you remember . . . ?"

But this was impossible. With us, every boy is regarded as having died in the course of initiation, which is undergone at the age of about fifteen. He must forget his childhood as soon as he has been brought in contact with the magic powers emanating from his ancestors. His head is shaved, he is bathed in cold water, and his blanket is burned; he must leap over obstacles and so learn that he is to separate himself from his past life. He is whipped, he sleeps on the bare ground, he is roused at night to submit to complicated tests, while learning from the mouths of elders the traditions, songs, and dances. When he leaves the school at about eighteen years of age, with a new name and blanket, he has indeed wiped out the past; therefore I could remind Amérique of nothing. If I'd dared to ask him, "Do you remember the mudfish, and *So* and *Afan?*" he would have denied it and been deeply outraged.

I woke him with quite a different question.

"Do you know Kankwe, Madame Docteur's Moba cook?"

Round us, Waji rustled unseen wings. Amérique, rubbing his eyes, repeated, "Kankwe? I've seen him. What of it? He's only a cook—an underling. *I'm* the king's stick-bearer."

The unseen beings hovered about Waji with sighs and lamentations. Again I shook Amérique, on his yellow mat.

"You know him slightly, don't you? I want you to get to know him better."

"Why?" he asked languidly, his eyes closed.

"I want him to be your *alenou-honton*—your 'close-friend-regarded-as-a-brother.' "

"Why, how can he help me?" growled Amérique, half asleep.

"We'll think about that later. See more of Kankwe: he'll burst with pride to have a stick-bearer taking an interest in him. Make him a few presents. Then one day you must say to him: 'It's time for us to consecrate our friendship according to ritual, so as to be assured of each other's loyalty and discretion.' Since you're the one to make the request the ceremony must take place in your hut. And as soon as the famous phrase has been spoken: 'I count on you in any fight with my enemies,' you must tell him at once what it is you need his help for."

"And what is it?" demanded Amérique, raising himself on his mat in great displeasure, a crease of suspicion between his brows.

"Promise you'll do it first, and then I'll tell you."

"Why should I promise what a woman asks me?" he said with all the ancient racial contempt for our sex. "You can't play about with the blood pact. You're asking me to tread a path full of pitfalls, and I can't answer before knowing what it is you're after, Doéllé. The blood pact's no joke."

But I leaned on his shoulder with the abandonment of Madame Docteur in the cemetery. I kissed him in the way Flavien had taught me, and my voice, like that of white people, held promise: "Say yes, say yes, Amérique—and one day I'll marry you. I swear it!"

"Yes," he said in a low voice as he seized me fiercely.

> *The sworn friend—did you know?—*
> *Should not be confused with the sponger*
> *Who comes to your house*
> *For what he can get to drink.*
> *Let us then not laugh at friendship*
> *For the true friend is readily discerned.*

This is what I repeated silently, while Amérique lost himself and memory of the world in me. It is the fine

154

poem that sworn friends recite at the burial of one of their brotherhood. And I thought of the blood pact, revealed to men by the genius of trees and animals, named *Aziza*. Like warriors and hunters, our former kings lost no time in surrounding themselves with sworn friends: discreet and devoted men whom they sent as spies, *agba-jigbeto*, into enemy country. Wearing round their necks a young palm shoot in token of submission, the *agba-jigbeto* said to the fetisher: "The bluebird that fears bush fires takes refuge in the cotton field among cool yellow flowers. I, unhappy, come to seek peace in the shadow of your fetish. Receive me! I will stay for three moons and will sweep the courtyard every morning."

During these three months the king's sworn friend listened and looked. He drew up a detailed plan of the town. His *grigris* shed about him discord and disease. But he was also furnished with amulets to halt the evil so cunningly brought about, and when he left, it was with the gratitude of his hoodwinked hosts. He then returned to his king primed with precious intelligence, having often made a blood pact with those on whom he spied.

Even today the blood pact, *Zodudu*, remains the most terrible of occult forces. It is a huge freemasonry with unsuspected ramifications, and its adepts are distinguished by no external sign. Few Africans devote themselves to great causes without assuring themselves of the discretion, loyalty, and devotion of their friends by entering into the blood pact with them. But *Zodudu* is not for great enterprises only. The father of a family who wants to keep the fidelity of his wives, or who fears betrayal by his servants or poisoning by his heirs, says to them one day, "*Mi na nou vodoun:* we will drink the fetish." He then enumerates crimes that would inevitably bring disaster on the house: does not a breaker of oaths go mad and eat his own excrements? Does he not swell up in a hideous manner? Does he not undergo ruin, fire, drowning, sickness, or imprisonment? And when he dies is it not carrion eaters alone that give him burial —in their own bellies?

I knew that two friends could also enter into the blood pact for their own personal advantage. They swear to help one another to build a hut or fashion a *grigri,* or to lend a hand with robbery, escape, or even murder. I should have liked to question him further on this subject, but he was already asleep. He slept a great deal after his initiation, convinced that sleep was necessary to him for the accomplishment of certain occult tasks. But I, who ever since Christmas night had acquired the depressing habit of lying open-eyed in the darkness, continued to listen to the vibrations of the unseen ones of Waji. Against my cheek I could feel the scarf of gold and pearls that belongs to the goddess of the winds, *Dan Anyidohuedo,* the fugitive and wanderer. I plainly felt the breath of *Ya,* the inconstant spouse of the thunder-god. From time to time I heard the roar of *Gu,* the fetish of swift executions. The whole little town of Waji vibrated like the string of some instrument. I listened and recited the end of the poem:

When he hears that fever has laid me low
My sworn friend will run to my side;
Of this I am sure.
My merest headache will make him anxious;
That is clear.
And when the day of the great departure comes,
Sworn friend, faithful friend, true friend,
You alone will show a quite particular devotion.
Let us then not laugh at friendship
For the true friend is readily discerned.

But the murmuring sounds of the southern night were giving place to the cool silence of morning. How pleasant it was, suddenly! I stretched like a cat—a cat that has not slept.

"Everything's going well," I thought to myself. "It's true that Amérique has a fickle temperament; his greatest enthusiasms fade and die unless constantly goaded. But what of it! I can always revive him and reawaken his interest. But I must get him to act quickly, as soon as Kankwe returns; for with Amérique a distant goal is a forgotten one."

Gently I tickled the stick-bearer's ears.

"Come on, wake up! And don't forget, Amérique—last night you said yes."

"I said yes? What about?"

He made a cowardly pretense of having forgotten and gazed at me innocently.

"You know quite well: Kankwe, Madame Docteur's cook!" I returned severely. "You gave me your word last night. A man can't go back on his word when his name is Amérique. You'll make a blood pact with him or I won't marry you."

Without another word I draped my green blanket about me, knotted a mauve *madras* about my head, and stepped haughtily over the threshold of the hut.

"Wait, Doéllé!" cried Amérique. "I'll do as you say if you'll marry me. But what is it I have to ask Kankwe?"

"Oh, nothing really. Just a little favor. Listen: every morning Madame Docteur drinks a glass of coconut milk. She drinks it alone in Capitaine Docteur's bungalow. Simply ask Kankwe to—" I bent over Amérique and whispered a few words in his ear.

"Doéllé!" he cried. And I went away laughing at his amazement.

The driver of a Syrian truck brought me to the maternity clinic in twenty minutes.

10

A di mu le na kê n'avo wo.

(Soap will not wash away the hostility of
the robe.)

THE white people returned a week later from that
searing expedition to the bush, thinner and with drawn
features.

Their car drew up in front of the hospital on a Sunday about noon. I saw them get out; their cheeks were
hollow; they seemed crushed by some destiny whose
approach not even Capitaine Docteur, usually so strong,
could hinder. They were dusty and seemed to have
emerged from the bush fires, drunk with black smoke,
flames, and ash.

I knew that on his return from the north Flavien
would forbid me ever to enter his house again. This must

have been agreed between him and Urgèle long before they left Manoho.

"Doéllé isn't an ordinary *évoluée*," the magistrate may have told her. "I can't just throw her out, or she might be dangerous. Leave it to time. And darling, don't be jealous—she's only a Negress, after all. I'll get rid of her for good and all when we come back from the north."

I was sure of this, and was not at all surprised when Amedéwovoé came to tell me with a wink that his master wanted to see me at once.

I took off my nurse's overall, adjusted my blanket—the one adorned with hearts and penknives (*dsen onmôo nê:* one must adorn oneself to please!)—and took the cemetery road. The harmattan was striding on Manoho, and already a dry, dancing mist softened the sharp outline of the palms.

Passing by the tomb of my Uncle Gamélé I paused to set down between the pillars a cake of cornmeal: my aunt had asked me to do this for her. She could not get as far as the cemetery that week and had said to me: "Lay a cake on Gamélé's tomb. He'll send you his thanks and blessing from beyond. A well-fed man is better disposed than a hungry one, be he dead or alive."

To please my aunt I laid this cake on the slab opposite the colored statue of Gamélé, and was just straightening up when the indignant voice of a white man made me start: "Doéllé! I thought you were a good Christian, and here you are feeding the dead like any other savage. Aren't you ashamed—you who were brought up in the faith of God—ashamed to revert like this to the customs of your country?"

It was the Reverend Father, the one who said Mass every Sunday at Manoho church. I could easily have explained and cleared myself by telling him that I was doing this as a courtesy to my aunt; yet some impulse of bravado made me stare him in the face without answering.

"I shall tell Mother Saint-Ange," he went on. "She'll be most distressed to learn that you bring food to the dead like a savage—a barbarian!"

"Indeed, a savage? A barbarian?" I repeated, indignant in my turn, taking a step toward the white cassock. "Do you know what you're saying, Father? In the Missions Africans are told about families in France who spend money at All Saints, filling their cemeteries with carnations and chrysanthemums. So the Catholic religion admits that dead people love the smell of carnations and the color of chrysanthemums. Well then, if your dead have a nose to smell with and eyes to see, you must please allow ours to have teeth for eating."

Speechless, the Reverend Father swung round on his heel and went.

Why was I so rude to him? Why? Ask the lagoon, ask the harmattan, ask the twelve months of the year. . . . My hands were still trembling as I walked up the steps of the courthouse. It was lunchtime. Flavien was sitting at the table, naked to the waist and radiating freshness from a recent shower. He was reading the letters that had come while he was away. Amedéwovoé

161

glided in barefooted and noiseless with a little dish of smoked shrimps and a pawpaw cut into slices.

"I sent for you, Doéllé," said Flavien, coming straight to the point, "to tell you that everything is over between us. Over, do you understand?"

Seated there behind his wooden table he used the stern voice of a judge. Oh, how like a judge you were, Flavien! Fine wrinkles that I did not know nevertheless humanized his frozen face a little.

"That's a reasonable decision," I answered. "I'll go, then, without bothering you any more."

He looked surprised, vaguely uneasy. He had expected tears, entreaties, threats, and instead he found on my face resignation, humility, and submission. His narrowed eye seemed to be asking: "What's behind this unnatural meekness?" His mouth tightened and was marked at the corners by a line of suspicion; it seemed to say: "Take care, Doéllé! If you're plotting some ugly little revenge I shall be able to take care of myself."

He resumed his meal as if I had ceased to exist. He shelled a shrimp and opened an airmail envelope, and would have seemed altogether at his ease but for the knee that fidgeted nervously beneath the table.

"Of course," he added, without raising his eyes, "I'll compensate you."

"Flavien, don't insult me!" I replied with excessive gentleness. "You've given me enough happiness these past two years to leave me rather in *your* debt."

And I left him.

"Women! To hell with women!" I could fancy him

162

growling when I'd gone. "All they're good for is to complicate life with worries and doubts and fuss."

The next day, however, he was no longer in the mood to damn all women to hell. Urgèle rang him up in the late afternoon to tell him that Capitaine Docteur had left for the Chopo dispensary. An hour alone after a fortnight of fever—what a windfall for lovers! They lost their heads, threw prudence to the winds, neglected the most elementary precautions and decided to drive together to a neighboring resthouse.

All this was reported to me minute by minute. I can imagine them even now speeding along in the car where they had so lately sat in a tormented company of three. I can hear their conversation broken by the noise of the engine, I can see Flavien acknowledging by a hasty gesture the greetings of natives along the roadside as they respectfully bared the upper part of their bodies.

Meanwhile I had hastened to a sorcerer who dwelt behind the school on the other side of the lagoon. I put into his hand a worn sandal which had belonged to Flavien and which I clung to as a keepsake. He took a little brown powder from a calabash and placed it on his tongue, and at once a jet of vapor shot from his mouth. He sneezed three times, pronounced some incantations, and assured me that the two whites would never be lovers in fact.

They had shut themselves into the resthouse without shame. The fiber mattress was dank with mildew and the odor of unknown bodies. No sheets, of course. Yet Flavien laid the naked body of Urgèle on this stained cloth, not hesitating to subject her delicate skin to its contact. The old caretaker whom they had sent away with a tip assured me of this. Urgèle, accustomed to embroidered pillow slips, curtains, black lace, and scent! This almost derelict resthouse, this sordid haste—Flavien had nothing better to offer the woman he loved. He was wretched over this and apologized when he should have kissed, with the incurable mania of white people for mixing mental agony with their lovemaking.

The minutes slipped swiftly by, but here was none of the intoxication they had expected; they were not now aflame, as at their brief meetings between two *sekos* or at the twilit edge of a beach. Gone was the ardor that had consumed them on their journey in the north. They who had so desperately awaited this moment of solitude were parted suddenly by a high barrier. Urgèle's skin touched that of Flavien, yet remained inert and unresponsive; it had lost the scent, savor, and velvet touch of the day before—it was silk, paper, metal. Flavien clasped Urgèle to him but his arms held only a captive shade, not a creature of flesh and blood. Nothing but a wraith.

"I've so often told him I'm not like a real woman," thought Urgèle, shattered. "He just wouldn't believe me. No one listens when I say that—and yet Flavien can feel for himself this evening that I have no right to love."

Flavien began to talk of Paris, that mysterious Paris of nostalgic memory of which in earlier days he had shown me the detailed map. And through the caretaker's rather incoherent account I heard again the words he had pronounced long since, and images that had grown familiar.

"Promise me," he pleaded, "that one day we shall meet in Paris, just us two alone! I expect we shall have been planning the meeting for years. You'll be coming back from the New Hebrides perhaps, and I shall step ashore from the Madagascar mailboat—but how glorious it will be to meet again! I shall take you to some quiet little hotel—there's one I know of near the Gare de Lyon, in the rue Traversière. No one will come and knock at the door—no one will know who we are. Street noises will reach us—car horns, the cry of the glazier, and the voices of market women. An accordion will play for us and we'll open the window and throw down a few sous wrapped in paper. If you don't feel like coming down to the restaurant I'll dress and run out to buy rolls and ham and oranges and a bottle of Alsatian wine, and bring it to you in bed. Your hair will be all over the place and you'll look at yourself in the glass on the cupboard door and laugh. And the night will be long. . . . There won't be any accordion then—only the cheerful shouting of some drunk and the bicycles of the night police patrol. You will sleep close, close against me, but I shan't sleep—I shall be far, far too happy. I shall watch over your sleep and listen to your breathing; I shall watch for your waking, to see whether you look happy to find yourself in my arms. Urgèle . . . We can't make love like this, all in a hurry and on edge. For weeks I've been dying of desire for you—but here, touching your lovely skin, I'm suddenly ashamed.

I feel ugly and poor beside you—I want to hide. In Paris you wouldn't awe me so. . . . Promise me there'll be other times, Urgèle, a long, long way from here. In three months, perhaps, when you go back to France? Or not for ten years, when we've both wandered over different continents?" Flavien's voice was full of hopeless sorrow. "Answer me, Urgèle!"

But Urgèle did not answer. I believe she was crying.

It was time to go back. Urgèle slipped on her black, lace-trimmed chemise as dusk sank heavily over the resthouse. There was no electric light, only a candle stuck in a bottle. Urgèle's sandal had slipped behind the bed; as she groped for it she felt the warm fur of some unseen, lurking creature, and snatched back her hand with a cry. Flavien blew out the candle and they left the cheerless room, gingerly feeling with their feet for the steps that were engulfed in darkness, and holding their arms outstretched like blind people, lest they collide with the walls.

"We're late. I hope to God we don't have a breakdown—I hope we get back before Frantz!" murmured Urgèle, already preoccupied with her immediate worries—already sundered from the man she loved. Flavien started the engine and let it run for a while before letting in the gear.

"Au revoir, Urgèle . . . Good-by, my love," he said gravely, as if divining that never again would he see her alone.

They plunged into the night. The road was deeply furrowed; sometimes it undulated like corrugated iron, transmitting a hideous motion to the car. The eyes of cats flashed now and then from the bushes. "Quick— quick—hurry—we're late!" Urgèle drove her nails into Flavien's arm: a habit she had fallen into during the trip to the north.

"Look!" she said in a low voice.

The whole width of the road was barred by a python: a swelling in the middle of its body spoke of freshly devoured prey. They had to pull up to allow the god to pass, and Flavien quickly opened the door and sprang out.

"Flavien, for heaven's sake don't hurt it!" cried Madame Docteur in a tone of dread. "Some people here say that those things are emanations from the rainbow and that to kill them brings bad luck."

"I'm not going to kill it—I just wanted to have a look at the beast," said Flavien, returning to his seat.

The gleaming python had slipped slowly into the tall grass. The engine was still running and only a touch was needed to send them speeding, speeding over the ruts. "Hurry—hurry—faster still!" Flavien was not talking now; by jerking the wheel he avoided the worst pot- holes, or the wall of a hut looming suddenly out of the dark by the roadside, or a swerve into the sand. Urgèle, hunched up against the door, was no doubt thinking of the python that Frantz had killed, and of Doéllé who declared that Dangbé always claimed his revenge.

When Flavien set her down a hundred yards or so short of the hospital, Madame Docteur saw at once that her husband had come home; the office lamp was lit in

167

the veranda and the medical truck with its lights on stood at the foot of the steps. The boys told me that Capitaine Docteur, who had already bathed and changed, greeted Urgèle without comment, but that after dinner a violent scene occurred between them. Kankwe, Yaya, and Bokari had been banished to the kitchen by a man white with fury, so they could hear nothing of what passed. And I unluckily was in the maternity ward helping the midwife with a premature birth, so the veil of mystery was never lifted from this nocturnal drama, though it was evident that Capitaine Docteur had forbidden Urgèle to see Flavien again.

Next day the harmattan began blowing, in great dry gusts from the east. A veil of mist lay over the lagoon and fine dust filtered through the *sekos*, covering floors and furniture.

Soon nerves would become frayed throughout Manoho. For some time the sickness had been lurking, but so far had shown no severe symptoms: undue irritation with the boy, perhaps, when he was late with the hot water or had sliced the pineapple badly. It was just a malaise, a vague restlessness and ill humor. But in the houses the few interior doors took it into their heads to split and the leather blotting pads began to warp. In the doctor's living room the elephant's tusk split along a crack that recalled the ravages of the previous dry season. Wounds on the patients' legs in the hospital healed, it is true, but everyone now went in dread of the epidemics that follow in the wake of the harmattan. Had not the rumor reached us of cerebrospinal fever as far south as Attimogan, where two cases had been confirmed? The schoolmaster's little daughter, having heard grownups describing the symptoms of this illness and wanting to make herself interesting, complained from morning till night of headaches and stiffness at the back of the neck. Madame Elisabeth, distracted, ran to the hospital to ask Capitaine Docteur a string of silly questions; he sent her impolitely back to her fashion magazines and novels. For lack of other occupation she called on old Lambert, who informed her with appropriate shouts that—marvelous to relate—a bullock had been slaughtered in Manoho.

"But of course," put in the ex-nun acidly, "the D.O. kept the best of it for himself—the *filet mignon*. Scraps are good enough for us. Good meat for those in high places—for us traders, bones."

"And what about potatoes?" yelped Madame Elisabeth. "Tons of them arrived with the last boat, and everyone in the station was given a hundredweight—except me. I was allowed only half. Why? Ah, it's not as pleasant to be pretty and sought-after as one might think. Men are so petty! They take schoolboy revenge if one doesn't give in quickly enough to suit them."

As she spoke she cast angry glances at the D.O. who had just come in. Her nostrils quivered, she crossed and uncrossed her legs, and shook the bracelets that hid the white patches on her wrists. Despite the descriptions of her conjugal felicity, that she gave to all who would listen, I couldn't help thinking that what she needed

169

was a pair of strong arms to beat her and possess her. "A pity that colonial tradition forbids lovemaking with Negroes," she must have reflected; for more than once I had seen her eyes rest greedily on Amérique's pectoral muscles.

Conversation continued in the planter's house between these two unsatisfied, idle women, the ex-nun and the schoolmaster's wife.

"I feel a craving for flowers just now—I long to arrange them in vases," said the first. "If I were in France I would buy gladioli. I adore them."

"I don't wonder," retorted the other, "they're such silly, pompous flowers!"

"Have a little more porto, and try one of these cakes: they're shaped like snakes, and you're so full of venom!"

Such was their cordial repartee, but it drew from the opponent only curt little laughs. Everyone talked thus at this season, and it never came to anything. People simply shrugged their shoulders and said, "It's the harmattan!"

11

Akaga méwoa ta kolo tiké na amé o.

(The vulture can't give you a cure for
baldness. If he could he wouldn't be bald.)

AS IF protected by an invisible wall, Urgèle found
herself excluded from the depressing conversations that
were taking place during the dry season. It was long
since the other women in Manoho had called upon her,
though the men always found some excuse for stopping
at the doctor's bungalow. Except Flavien, that is; Urgèle had promised her husband not to see him again and
for all her bitter distress she kept her word. I remember
only a certain evening . . .

From the hospital I could hear the curt tones of Capitaine Docteur; he was reprimanding an assistant for in-
accuracy in measuring a dose of penicillin. I could guess

171

that he was pale, with the trace of his old sunburn on his forehead; I knew that his fists were clenched tight enough to split the skin; and to this new creature who had replaced the calm, controlled, even-tempered man I knew I said, *"Ema fio ho!* Don't burn!" For among us it is said that anger burns a man up inside.

At that moment the truck from the nurseries drew up before the house. The agricultural officer hastened up the steps and dashed onto the veranda where Urgèle, pale and thoughtful, was resting.

"Madame, I know you're a sensitive woman," he began without preamble. "You're the only person I can confide in. You know perhaps that I was a married man? My wife came out with me last time, and about a year ago we went home on leave. Her mother at once began to turn her against me, asking her whether she meant to waste her life and lose her looks in the colonies, or stay behind and help run the shop. I did what I could to dissuade her from this—I told her how easy colonial life was, with servants and cars and a better salary and a possibility of saving. The mother won. Two days before coming back here I applied for a divorce. I didn't want to feel I was married any longer; it's too much to bear when one's so far away. I asked for a divorce and today a letter came to tell me that it's through—I'm free, she's free. And I'm miserable. Madeleine can't be unfaithful to me any longer, can she, since she's ceased to be my wife?"

I believe Madame Docteur was not even surprised at the excitement that was consuming this usually so colorless man. He was sitting in the rattan chair once occupied by Flavien, and it was Flavien's voice that Urgèle was hearing: "One day you'll sleep close, close against me. I shan't sleep; I shall be far, far too happy. I shall listen to your breathing, I shall watch for you to wake, to see if you're glad to find yourself in my arms."

These were the words that Urgèle was listening to, not her visitor's melancholy recital. Her watch told her that it was six o'clock, and she must have remembered that it was at six o'clock she had joined Flavien in the cemetery among the rustling palms. At six she had drifted with him about the lagoon of the sacred alligators. At six they went walking on the deserted shore, and on their last evening they had tried to make love in a disused resthouse.

Unbearable that it should be six o'clock! But why did she feel so lacking in energy and courage? Why did she not run to the courthouse, calling out to Flavien, "I'm leaving Frantz! Let's get married!"? What lethargy held her captive to that divan, within wearisome sound of the breaking waves?

At the end of the veranda Amalia the mulatto sewed on, threading her needle with deliberation, stitching and then fixing her pale Teutonic eyes on the misty lagoon. With expressionless face she watched the agricultural truck move off and, immediately afterward, the D.O.'s car draw up at the foot of the steps.

"I was just going to the post," said the new arrival, ceremoniously kissing Madame Docteur's hand, "and ventured to look in and ask how you are. This harmattan—! I see it has affected you—you look worn out. This is our worst season; one can only take perpetual showerbaths and drink without stopping. Thank you, a whisky would be very welcome."

The D.O.'s features were drawn; his eyes alone were alive and burning in his gaunt face. Bokari, with a slight smirk, took out a bottle of iced water, and was hardly back in the kitchen before the other boys there burst out laughing. You would have thought they'd never seen anything so funny in their lives before. Dusk was already falling on the Konkomba helmets, the Sudanese esparto work and the stiff panther skins. Urgèle never thought of lighting the lamp.

"Oh Flavien, Flavien!" she groaned in her heart. "Where are you?"

"I implore you," the D.O. was saying in a low voice, "only let me love you! I alone could make you happy. You're smiling! Yes, you must often have heard those words before—but I mean them, because I've no longer any ambition—no ambition but to love you. People who chase after success, money, and fame are too busy to find words for what comes from the heart. A man must have passed through the fires of youth and be detached from all these material things if he's to understand and love you, Urgèle."

But now the heavy tread of Capitaine Docteur was heard on the steps; he seemed to have grown heavier these last weeks and he drank too much cognac. He looked as white as his uniform when he stepped onto the dark veranda, and showed such marked coldness to the visitor that the latter left at once. Before his car had begun to move Frantz exclaimed, "When's this ridiculous procession going to stop? On Thursday it was the schoolmaster, with his books of propaganda. Yesterday old Lambert and his cocoa, today that fool of an agricultural officer, and now, to crown all, the D.O. with his hand-kissing! Since you gave up seeing the magistrate you've been receiving altogether too many visitors. I've had enough of it, understand?"

Gone was the time when the doctor turned red and white by turns, repressing his feelings. He used simply to drum with his fingers when anything annoyed him, or else the muscle in his jaw began to quiver. Never had he shouted like this.

"But Frantz, I can't help it!" said Urgèle, in the voice of a child defending itself. "They just came; I couldn't send them away."

"Oh, of course! Nothing's ever your fault! One mustn't think of you as a woman—yes, I know all that by heart. But there are limits, even to fairy tales. You belong to the earth all right, Urgèle, and not the clouds. If you're a misfit it's because of your lack of balance, your neuroses, your—"

"Frantz, let me go away from here. Let me go back to France by the next plane."

"You'll go when I go, in ten weeks' time, and not before. You've caused enough scandal in Manoho without starting a fresh one. But that's you all over: as soon as you hear a few home-truths from me you talk of leaving. You want to run away—you simply can't look facts

175

in the face. All you can do is daydream, reality terrifies you. You like to think that yours is a soul above the common run, astray in a world unworthy of you. But I see you as a sick mind whose whims I've foolishly pandered to—until now. But now things will be different, Urgèle. I'm going to lay bare your own case to you, medically and surgically, and whether you want to or not you're going to listen. From now on *you* must give way to *me*, do you hear? Give way and obey!"

"Never. I'll divorce you first."

Capitaine Docteur seized his wife's wrists and twisted them. He shook Urgèle like a sapling and threw her roughly to the ground, where she remained on her knees, panting and slightly bent forward, with her widened eyes fixed upon her husband.

"I'll get a divorce," she said firmly. She had fallen at the exact spot on which the python had been killed at Christmas.

Capitaine Docteur, unrecognizable, leaped at her, grasping in his hand a rusty hunting knife which served him usually as a letter opener, but which had already slain a god. Swift as a gull Urgèle rose and fled toward the lagoon.

While Capitaine Docteur sank down on the divan with one hand over his eyes, his breath coming in gasps and cold sweat pouring off him, Amalia the mulatto placidly folded the napkin she had been embroidering. She drew her blanket up around her hips and walked away with her usual detached air: her day's work was done. Shouting, anger, passion were things incomprehensible to her, as children's games are to grown-up people. The winds of madness that had been blowing over Manoho since the coming of the harmattan could not reach Amalia. For the rest of her life she would be there, facing the lagoon, poised and still. Had not Madame Docteur once compared her to Lachesis, one of the three Fates who, indifferent to life's dramas, spin the thread of days?

It was the albino, the Child of the Moon, who afterward told me the story of the hunting knife; my turn of duty finished just when the D.O. came, and I went to Waji, whither Amérique had summoned me.

"It's done!" cried the stick-bearer as soon as he spied me in the distance. "When will you marry me, Doéllé?"

"Now then, steady! I don't know what you're talking about. What's done?"

That's what I said as I held him off, though for days I'd been waiting for just those words.

"It's done, I tell you," he repeated, lowering his voice. "The cook and I drank the fetish last night. When do we get married?"

"Well, well—you seem in a great hurry for your reward, Amérique. I'd quite forgotten that blood-pact business. There are so many other things on my mind at the maternity clinic."

I went on talking lightly, yet my heart was thumping at the thought that they had made this pact. But suddenly I said to him, and my voice trembled as I spoke, "Amérique, how can I be sure that you've really drunk the fetish with Kankwe? Tell me, tell me quickly!"

Confident that he was speaking to his future wife he abandoned reticence and told me that on the previous day he had collected strophanthus and bombax bark, and taken a handful of earth from before *Hebiesso's* temple; also a pigeon, a pig, some kernels of corn, and cotton, and a big stone for crushing and pounding; all these he had placed in his hut. Kankwe, dazzled at the thought of becoming the sworn friend of the royal stick-bearer, came at the hour agreed upon for the ceremony. They shut themselves up together in the hut and stood naked before a circle on the ground in which Amérique had rapidly drawn a warrior's knife, a crocodile, a gun, *Hebiesso's* ax, a gallows rope, a hobble, and a snake. This circle, somewhat hollowed, was the "pact hole." Amérique, having recited the disasters that would result from breaking the oath, crushed the bark and made a paste, mixing with it the sacred earth from before the temple. First the pig and then the pigeon had their throats cut by Kankwe, who added a few drops of their blood to the cake of earth and bark.

"And it was then," Amérique explained, "that each of us made a slight cut on the back of the other's hand, between thumb and first finger, and sucked each other's blood."

This drinking of blood was at one time sufficient guarantee of friendship, mutual aid, confidence, and devotion. It was only after certain sworn brothers shamelessly broke their word that the gods of sky, fire, water, smallpox, and war were invoked to bring death to the faithless.

"Then," went on Amérique in an ever lower, more hesitant tone, "we ate the cakes, and the *calalu* of concord. I poured out some gin and said to Madame Docteur's cook: 'You know the duties imposed by this pact? This fire which you're about to drink will burn you up if ever you are false to your oath! Destitution, madness, or death will attend the smallest breach.' And Kankwe said, 'We'll help each other, though it were to do harm to one of our kinsfolk!' And I said, 'We'll help each other, though it were to do harm to one of your masters, Kankwe!' "

"Amérique! And what did he say to that? Tell me quickly! My head's seething with impatience."

Amérique made no reply. He was drawing patterns with a stick on the floor of the hut and seemed annoyed at having said so much. The blood pact is a forbidden subject. Small wonder if so changeable a nature as Amérique's should cause him to break out angrily.

"What does it matter to you what he said? You know enough already. Don't worry: this morning Madame Docteur drank some rather special coconut milk; she'll drink more tomorrow, and the next day, and every day until—"

"Quiet, Amérique! I must go now. Good-by, and thank you."

But he held me back roughly by a fold of my blanket.

"You've forgotten the most important thing, Doéllé. When do we marry?"

"Not until I've seen some results," I answered. And I went out.

The night was alive with the cries of flying foxes. "Does Flavien still hate them?" I wondered with a smile, little guessing that just then, in Manoho, Capitaine Docteur was threatening Urgèle with a hunting knife. Why, after all, was Flavien so afraid of flying foxes? They're pretty things, delicate and soft. Madame Docteur once told me that my skin was soft as theirs. But this evening he's all alone, solitary as the agricultural officer in the experimental gardens. There's no one beside him to help him forget those piercing cries that remind him of joys beyond his grasp; to forget privation, devastating jealousy, and endless torment.

Amedéwovoé had told me that since his return from the north the magistrate had received no one in his bungalow—that he sat out on the terrace every evening and spent a great part of the night there, with a hurricane lamp behind him and a bottle of brandy within reach.

"He drinks and smokes furiously," Amedéwovoé told me, wagging his head. "He stares into the darkness without moving. Sometimes he talks to himself. He hasn't looked into a book for days and his letters from France aren't even opened."

But I didn't want to think of Amedéwovoé's depressing words any more. And indeed, what did it matter to me if Flavien succumbed to despair and drink because of a white woman whom he hadn't even possessed? I felt strangely released from my love and hate, now that destiny was following the path I had traced for it. I had no further cause to hesitate, or feel anxious, or brood.

Did I not know that one day Flavien would have to forget Urgèle?

While I was breathing the cool evening air in the streets of my childhood, Madame Docteur wandered by the lagoon; so the boys told me next day. She walked at random through the darkness, her shoulders bowed like those of an old woman. She must have felt bereft of youth and beauty and of hope after the fearful words that the doctor had shouted at her. Her whole attitude betrayed shame and distress. I was walking light-heartedly in Waji, while Urgèle in Manoho dragged heavy feet. I know her—I can guess at her thoughts; I know why she didn't run to the courthouse and call Flavien. She was afraid. She had not seen the magistrate since their last meeting in the resthouse, and was wondering anxiously whether he still loved her.

"My husband wanted to kill me! Protect me—keep me—keep me always!" She might have said this to him instead of walking alone on the shores of the lagoon. But she was afraid he might look down at her, narrowing his right eye.

Worn out with bitterness and grief Urgèle went back. What else could she do? Fate had decided that she should in no way escape the python's vengeance. She must return to her husband's house and there, for many mornings to come, drink the coconut milk specially prepared for her by Kankwe, which little by little would deprive her of strength and lead her by a path of ever-increasing anguish to her death.

I walked on through the alleyways of Waji until I reached the public place where the "drum" was in full swing.

Since studying medicine in Dakar I had not attended a single one of these; such things seemed ill-suited to my new education and my status as *évoluée*. I wonder what malignant spirit led me there that evening. Great animation pervaded the crowd that was gathered around two young men, representing the male and female incarnations of the fetish *Hebiesso*, god of thunder and lightning. One leaped like a tiger with foaming lips and savage eyes; the other moved with hanging arms and lowered lids as if held in some lethargy. The moonlit scene had the quality of hallucination. The smell of black skins intensified with the crescendo of the cowrie-covered gourds. Océa my sister was there with her friends; she was wearing her soft velvet cloth with the stripes. So intent was she on the rhythmical waving of her handkerchief that she didn't see me, but I fancied that the fetisher Agbatakbato, the Man-of-God-in-the-Empty-Room, fixed his burning looks upon her. Was this illusion? No. His eyes never left Océa. A woman overcome by sleep fell captive to the fetish, then an old hag began rolling on the ground in convulsions; these two were carried out of the ring, followed by the envious eyes of others who also sought to fall asleep. Agbatakbato paid no attention to the toothless crones who sank to the ground, and took little interest in Sossou, the male incarnation of *Hebiesso*, who continued his wild capers and rushed in to butt *Sacripé*, the female incarnation, who was now raving. Agbatakbato looked fixedly at Océa.

"Resist him! Don't let yourself be enslaved!" I cried silently to my sister. "Get away at once!"

She went on waving her handkerchief in time to the beat, but suddenly I saw her gasp. Her naked torso was shaken with trembling, her eyes rolled upward and she fell upon the ground. The fetisher gave a smile of triumph, then turned slowly toward me and regarded me challengingly.

"Ho, ho!" he seemed to be saying. "There in the dust lies the sister of the proud nurse! What does this haughty stranger, this disdainful *évoluée* from Manoho, think of fetishes and fetishers now?"

Silence had fallen over the place. All were watching me to see how I would take it, fancying perhaps that I would leap into the circle to drag my sister from humiliation. My instinct impelled me to it, but I controlled myself; for Océa was already rising, covered with red dust, with sweat on her forehead and slavering lips. Alas, she ran not to me but to the priest, and lay humbly at his feet. She babbled incoherently; she was in subjection, she surrendered herself to the fetish. I looked at her in amazement. Was Océa the arrogant vanquished —she who had so often laughingly declared herself beyond the reach of witchcraft—she who never attended a "drum" except to dance and amuse herself? How often, even, she had joked about our mother and Fossou her lover, because one bowed before pythons and the other refused honey to please his fetish! Océa, frivolous Océa, who did not believe in God and grew daily more remote from native cults—Océa was now but a helpless girl blindly obeying the silent orders of a fetisher.

The drum began again with violence, and powerfully muscled men took up their positions near Fossou to restrain him; for now in his frenzy he was attempting to dash his head against the trunks of the teak trees. The gourds with their nets of cowries were once more in frantic agitation, and women began to sing and scream and move their arms and shoulder blades in an effort to attain the revolting ecstasy that had overtaken Océa. Sickened, I slipped away into the night, far from the noise, far from this hideous scene.

"Laugh away—laugh at the ancient customs of your country!" the Waji initiates seemed to be crying. "Your pretty sister Océa is ours, for all that. Did you see her bite the dust? Did you see her rolling eyes—her breasts muddied with red earth? Did you see her kiss the feet of the fetisher?"

And an unknown, ironic, scornful voice whispered in my ear: "But you, Doéllé, who go to church on Sundays—haven't you resorted to the blood pact to slake your thirst for vengeance?"

I glanced around in fear. No one had followed me. Waji was deserted. It was only a voice, a mouthless, tongueless voice. Waji was alive with voices that called from the shadows, as I knew. It was not the first time that I had heard the breath of the unseen; but now a shudder of fear ran through me.

Some time before, Amérique had given me a protec-

tive *grigri* which he had made specially for me from
the eye of a duck, the tail of a lizard, and three blades
of the magic grass called *tingbé*. Scorning this amulet
I had tossed it into a corner of my mother's hut; now I
ran to find it and held it between my hands all night.

12

Ado me sogbe ye pona Agbodja.

(The Agbodja drum plays only when
concord prevails.)

CEREBROSPINAL meningitis made its insidious
way southward. This fever first appeared in our country ten years ago, and ever since then it has remained
dormant during the rains, to wake in December in epidemic waves that increase in violence for six months.
But it was unknown on the coast, and confined itself
to the north. It was one of the northern products, like
millet and elephants and Konkomba warriors.

When Capitaine Docteur isolated five patients at
Waji, the white people of Manoho began to show
concern. They regarded as normal the eight thousand
cases round Yama-Laka, high up and far away among

186

the rocks and bush fires, but the five in Waji seemed to them a personal insult and a direct threat. Think of it! A disease well established in the north daring to thrust its tentacles down to the sea. Who could have dreamed of such impudence?

"An Akposso has just come into hospital," Capitaine Docteur told Urgèle one morning. "We isolated him at once. His symptoms are suspicious: curvature, head-ache, and stiffness at the back of the neck. Can the disease have reached Manoho, I wonder?"

But Urgèle seemed indifferent to this peril, as indeed she had been to everything for some days past. This once so elegant woman no longer displayed her Paris gowns. From morning till night she wore the white wrapper with the wide sleeves, and left her hair undone. Stretched on the divan in the veranda she gazed, like Amalia the mulatto, at the lagoon. Her voice, once so intense, was now no more than a murmur, and she pushed away the stuffed crabs, roast pork, and guavas. Nothing, I assure you, but her daily glass of coconut milk seemed to please her now.

"A Nago woman has just been brought in," said Capi-taine Docteur at lunchtime. "When she sits it's impos-sible to straighten her legs in a line with her thighs, and unfortunately that's one of the signs of cerebrospinal fever."

But Urgèle went on peeling her green orange with-out replying, and the doctor began to feel uneasy at this prolonged apathy.

"Perhaps I was too severe with her; she's so easily

187

hurt," he may have thought. "I made no allowances for a sensitivity that feels the effects of any scene long after it's over. This depression dates from the evening when I threw her down and threatened her with the knife. It was a bit melodramatic, certainly, but she was driving me mad with her absurd magazine-story behavior. I should like to comfort her now and make her feel that she can lean on me—but how am I to say it? I don't know any of the words that she'd like to hear."

With all his thoughts bent upon the stranger peeling her orange, Capitaine Docteur tried to talk her language. But Urgèle looked up at him with eyes emptier than empty rooms and he gave up hope of being understood. He repressed his anxiety with an irritated shrug and must have said to himself: "Why seek a mental cause? Her depression's due to the harmattan. She's tired, as we all are just now. In another eight weeks we shall be on our way to France and she'll have got back her strength. There's nothing to be done for her now but to double her dose of quinine."

And he went out. He was going to make a lumbar puncture in each of the patients, and so obtain proof of the disease if it was there. The results were positive; cerebrospinal fever had reached Manoho. Drumming his fingers on the desk, Capitaine Docteur had a talk with the nursing orderlies, instructing them in the quantity of sulpha drugs to be given, and then went to see the schoolmaster who was suffering from a bout of malaria and loudly demanding a quinine injection.

"Good afternoon, sir. My master's waiting for you,

my-good-master-who-came-to-Africa-to-educate-the-Negroes-for-a-mere-pittance."

It was Marit's boy who thus greeted the doctor as he stepped from the medical van. This ignorant young Kotokoli knew only one sentence in French; the schoolmaster had made him learn it by heart and the boy conscientiously repeated it parrotwise to every caller. But Capitaine Docteur was in a very bad temper; he was thinking of the meningitis and the steps to be taken, and in the ovenlike heat that quivered over the schools the little bag he carried seemed of leaden weight. Roughly he pushed the boy aside and entered the schoolmaster's bungalow, resolved to refuse any drink and to go back to the hospital as soon as the injection had been given. "I won't be delayed by Madame Elisabeth's idiotic chatter," he must have said to himself. "No, I refuse to be held up here."

But Madame Elisabeth was taking a siesta with her daughter. Only old Lambert who had come to pay a friendly call was sitting beside Marit's long chair; they were engaged in an animated conversation which they broke off abruptly on the doctor's entrance. The schoolmaster's cook described the scene to me.

"Well, Doctor!" roared the cassava planter, his white hair more on end than ever. "What about these two suspect cases?"

"What—have you heard about them already?" exclaimed the doctor in surprise, with an aggressive lift of his eyebrows.

"Everyone knows everything in Manoho. So it's cerebrospinal, eh?" said the schoolmaster, his broad face gleaming with sweat and anxiety.

"I've just made the lumbar punctures and there's no possible doubt. The spinal fluid is cloudy and swarming with diplococci."

"We're in for an epidemic; I've been expecting this for the past ten days. Are we in any danger?"

The schoolmaster had quite forgotten his malaria and had no need of the quinine injection.

"In theory the European has nothing to fear from it," said Capitaine Docteur in his most professional manner. "With gargling and nasal douches of gomenol, infection can be avoided. When possible, of course, it's as well to limit contact with the natives."

"Limit contact! Quite so—and what about my schools? They won't be closed until the epidemic has assumed the same proportions as in the north. And in the meantime—?"

"But the disease isn't so fearsome as you seem to think, Marit. When they're treated in time, Africans usually recover easily. The trouble is that they often come to the dispensary too late. They're unwilling to trust the doctors until the fetishers have shown that they can do nothing for them. By that time they can't open their mouths to swallow *thyasomides*, so that they must be given serum injections—"

"But tell me, Doctor," broke in the planter rudely, "don't you think it's rather queer the way this disease has come down south? It's never happened before. It makes one wonder whether people coming back here from Yama-Laka brought it with them. When you were in the north you didn't of course go into any of the infected areas?"

"Certainly I did," snapped the doctor, resuming his aggressive air.

"What! But it's forbidden! You as a doctor should know that better than anyone. Yet instead of setting an example you abused your professional privilege by taking your wife and the magistrate into the forbidden zone. Do you realize your responsibility in this matter?"

The planter's bellowings resounded through the bungalow, and the schoolmaster, who was attempting to express his own opinion, could not make himself heard. Capitaine Docteur, white with anger, stepped right up to old Lambert shouting, "Are you preferring a charge against me? Then appeal at once to the Governor. It was he who authorized my journey."

With that he swung around and went out. On his return to the hospital he was still seething with rage.

Next day two fresh cases occurred at Manoho. It was a Sunday. Leaning on her elbows beneath a raised *seko* Madame Docteur was gazing at the lagoon; her full, white sleeves drooped like the wings of dead gulls. Beyond, at the courthouse, Flavien was pacing up and down the terrace. He was thin and tense, with deep lines at the corners of his mouth, and for some days he had terrified the natives by the pitiless severity of his sentences. While Capitaine Docteur silently tended the meningitis cases, the other white people as they came from Mass conferred together in low tones. I left them to their troubles and being off duty I went to Waji where Amérique had arranged to meet me.

On the way I met Océa and my heart contracted; I had not spoken to her since the evening when she had rolled in the dust at Agbatakbato's feet. She was unaware that I had seen her humiliation and I was careful not to tell her.

"*Eso bedo*, Doéllé!" she cried gaily. "Are you coming to see us?"

"No, not today, Océa. I've got to see Amérique."

"Do come, just for a little. If you like I'll do your hair."

I reflected quickly that I was early for my appointment and that if Océa did my hair she might perhaps talk about the "drum," and so I said affectionately, "You know I always give in to you. Do my hair, then."

We sat down in my mother's hut, Océa on a rickety stool and I on the ground between her knees, with bent head. She began to divide my hair into innumerable squares and to oil each lock. This Abongo style of mine takes three hours to do. Incapable as she was of sustained mental activity, Océa gladly spent time on whatever flattered her vanity and gave her the feeling of being immediately useful. Suddenly she broke off, comb suspended, eyes blank.

"Well, Océa? Are you already tired of making me beautiful?"

She looked down at me with a troubled air.

"I'm sorry, Doéllé. I don't know what's the matter with me. These last few days I've seemed to hear someone calling me, and yet there's never anyone about. At night too someone calls, 'Océa! Océa!' and I don't know who's speaking. Then I fall asleep again and dream always the same dream: I leave Mother and you, Doéllé, I leave Fossou and I get into a pirogue, taking nothing with me; you stay behind and I don't know where I'm going, but I feel it's a long way off. What does the dream mean, do you know, Doéllé?"

Alas, I knew only too well. A shudder ran through me, but I answered briskly, "You eat cassava at night—that's why you have these absurd dreams, Océa. Come on, hurry up and finish my hair, or Amérique will be cross with me for being late."

And indeed Amérique was getting very impatient.

"Have you fixed a day for our wedding?" he asked at once. "You asked me to do something for you and I've done it. Now it's your turn to keep your promise."

"I'm waiting for a definite result, Amérique. When I've got what I want I'll marry you, but not before."

He became angry and spoke very sharply. With word and caress I tried to soften him, but my mind was still anxiously with Océa. I saw her sitting upright in her pirogue, setting forth alone without friends or baggage, on the great journey of death. . . . Suddenly a piercing shriek sounded over Waji, a woman's cry: "Ee-woo!"

I leaped to my feet. In all the doorways black, startled

193

faces appeared. I ran full tilt to my mother's hut, followed by the whole village. The shriek continued ever more faintly through the twilight: "Ee-woo!"

"Océa has been carried off by the fetish!" yelled a man. "I saw her. There was a chalk drawing in front of her hut. She was coming back from a walk with Fossou and stepped accidentally into this circle. She seemed paralyzed for a moment, and then she gave a frightful scream and ran away without seeming to recognize anybody."

"She's run to the *Hebiesso* cult house! I saw her too," cried a woman. "Agbatakbato was waiting for her on the doorstep, smiling. She'll become a fetish priestess now."

"Océa, Océa!" my mother was sobbing. "Have you insulted the fetish? Or why have you been snatched from me?"

"We were to be married," groaned Fossou. "When shall I see her again? For three years she'll be away from me."

Stricken with horror and grief I found nothing to add to the chorus of lamentations. In our country certain girls are vowed to the service of the fetish from birth; others enter the cult house of their own free will; others again who have offended a fetish are punished by him and dragged away into his service. But Océa? For a moment the unbearable thought struck me that the wrathful *Vodoun* had turned upon my sister the vengeance intended for me.

"No, it can't be! The gods care nothing for white

people. What does it matter to them if I give slow poison to Madame Docteur? This kidnapping has been arranged by Agbatakbato alone," I told myself vehemently. "The fetish network needs adepts from every great family, and Agbatakbato has chosen Océa because she's beautiful and will enhance the prestige of his school. And isn't she also the sister of a puffed-up Catholic nurse who studied medicine in Dakar?"

I mingled my tears with those of my mother. We both knew Océa's laziness and pride: how would she endure the stern conventual discipline that was to lead her, passively consenting, to initiation? All she loved in life was dancing and love-making and being paid compliments; from now on she would live in solitude. She had always followed her own whims; now for three years she must obey Agbatakbato, the Man-of-God-in-the-Empty-Room. She had rubbed her skin with coconut fiber and anointed her body with scents and cosmetics; now she would be tattooed on back and breast, she would be whipped, she would sleep on the bare ground.

"We were to have been married," repeated Fossou, crushed by this blow. "I had asked her mother for her twice. Now what are we to do?"

It was true that my sister was no virgin. She could not have shown her family, on pain of sterility, the little bloodstained handkerchief called *hunvo*. She could not claim those bracelets of blue beads called the virgin's reward, given by a husband to his bride in recognition of her maidenhood. But she might have become the happy mistress of a house with the right of supervision over other wives whom Fossou would not have failed to take soon afterward. Now she was torn from family life and would remain absent from us for three years. *Hebiesso* had marked her for his servant—*Hebiesso*, the terrible lord of thunder and lightning.

This god, the creator of the celestial arch, is held in great awe by the Minas; he is represented in the form of a double-bladed ax and by a strip of iron twisted like a snake. Woe to the one he chooses for his victim! Should lightning strike the thatched roof of a hut, the householder is burdened with fines by the Achinassi fetishers who claim that he must have committed some crime unknown to men. Should a woman be struck during a tornado she is condemned to execution; no one may touch her body, which is exposed ignominiously on a hurdle, like that of a criminal.

"*Hebiesso, Hebiesso!*" I prayed as I returned with hanging head to the maternity clinic. "Don't harm Océa. She's innocent—and so beautiful!"

.For the next two days I forgot about meningitis and Urgèle and Flavien, and thought only of my young sister shut up in the cult house. What would they give her to eat? For three years she would not be allowed to cook her own food or buy the smallest thing for herself; an old *Hebiesso* priestess would prepare her meals. Was she able to sleep on the bare ground? How was she enduring the silence and solitude to which she was committed? The greasy oil of the fetish priestesses was already on her body, and two yards of unbleached cotton had replaced her velvet blankets. Soon she would begin to learn veneration for ancestors and to absorb a spirit of unity and discipline; then would follow the ritual dances of homage to *Hebiesso*, and chants in a special language.

On the third day at dusk, when Capitaine Docteur was leaving for Waji dispensary, I asked to go with him. Together we visited the hut where the meningitis cases were housed, not far from the *Hebiesso* convent, and I said to myself as I surveyed the wall dividing my sister from the everyday world, "Océa lives behind that red wall and I can't see her. She lives and breathes so near to me, and yet she's further away than if she were at sea. Was that dream of hers, that I took as a premonition of death, no more than a foreshadowing of this isolation and the loneliness of the cult house?"

Capitaine Docteur, who was in a very somber mood, exchanged a few brief words with the nurses and inspected temperature charts and treatment cards; there were now nine cases of cerebrospinal meningitis in Waji. Suddenly I trembled: a few girls were coming out of the convent, one behind the other, their pitchers upside down on their heads. Among the novices, sternly guarded by an old *Hebiesso* priestess, a *Sossi*, walked Océa with her head shaved. I knew that it is forbidden to talk to novices; that indeed one must pretend not to see them and lower one's eyes as they pass. But a desperate impulse made me follow the procession all the way to the fountain and my heart cried out wildly:

"Océa, Océa! Leave those women and come with me! Danger hangs over your shaven head. Come, and I'll protect you."

On reaching the fountain I could not resist touching my sister's arm to attract her attention; but the novices looked at me indignantly and the old woman drew near with an air of menace.

"*Baba dé*, I beg your pardon," I murmured, while Océa remained with bowed head apparently unconscious of my intrusion into her new life. In my agitation I had forgotten that to address these girls, even in apology for having touched them accidentally, is forbidden; and at the sound of my voice the old woman sprang at me, her claws out, her face distorted with fury. In front of Océa, who remained unseeing, the old priestess was on the point of scratching my face, snatching off my *doukou* and tearing my nurse's overall. Capitaine Docteur's intervention alone saved me from a humiliating brawl which would have brought all the initiates down upon us.

"Doéllé, what's going on here? The truck's waiting to take us back to Manoho."

He asked no further questions, and the procession of novices returned to the cult house beneath the vengeful eye of the old woman. The doctor had too much on his mind to be inquisitive about a dispute between his nurse and a fetisher. At Manoho only three new cases had been confirmed, but fear haunted the white people. Madame Elisabeth fulminated against Urgèle all day long.

"Very pleasant, no doubt," she said acidly, "to tour the north between one's husband and one's lover, but unfortunately it is we who must suffer the consequences. If she had stayed quietly at home like any normal wife, we should have had nothing to fear. Do you feel any stiffness at the back of your neck, my treasure? You're sure you have no headache, angel?" she asked her daughter.

The agricultural officer had never felt so content to be among his coffee bushes and his nut-shelling machines. He never came near the markets without a handkerchief soaked in disinfectant under his nose. Old Lambert and the schoolmaster sought immunity in rum. The D.O.'s wife had put away her beige and brown woollies, her clicking needles and her raffia bag, and gave herself up to fear with a thrill of enjoyment. The atmosphere of muffled silence that accompanies epidemics, or even the threat of them, restored to her an energy she had long lost. Her husband protested strongly but in vain: she continued to receive callers armed with an atomizer, and with or without their good will they were obliged to undergo a spray of gomenolized oil.

The day after my meeting with Océa, a white man from the north arrived in Manoho. For a moment the station was paralyzed: who would ask this microbe-carrier to lunch? Who would dare offer a meal and a shower to this diplococcus-soaked traveler? The freest, most openhanded hospitality prevails in the colony when visiting white people are concerned: no introductions or cards are needed. A man is white: reason enough to

kill the plumpest fowl, to open the last of the tinned
food, to make enthusiastic offers of medicine, a thermos,
a Hausa hat, a camp bed or, if he wants it, lifelong hospitality. That the whites of Manoho hesitated even for an
instant to obey this rule showed how strong a gust of
madness had indeed blown through them.

"You needn't appear if you'd rather not. Stay in your
room," said the D.O. to his wife. "I shall receive this
Assistant District Officer at once at the Residency."

And the traveler, who was used to living in the very
heart of the epidemic and who had made his way for
weeks along roads cluttered with meningitics, marveled
at the terror prevailing in Manoho.

"How do you manage to avoid the disease in Yama-
Laka?" asked the D.O.'s wife, who had stuffed her nostrils with cotton wool and kept at a prudent distance
from her guest.

"Madame, the first time I used gomenol was on arriving here."

"Do you mean you don't attempt to guard against
infection?" she exclaimed in a hollow voice. "But they
say there are eighty new cases a day."

"That's true enough, but I'm a fatalist. Whatever one
may do, one can't alter the hour of one's death by a
single second; and so instead of wasting time in useless
precautions I simply double my ration of cognac."

During this conversation the D.O. who had just had
an altercation with Flavien, was writing a long report to
the Governor. He felt that a magistrate who neglected
his work to go touring the north and bringing back the

microbes of cerebrospinal fever should be promptly and severely dealt with. He little guessed that the Governor on receiving this missive three days later would crumple it into a ball and throw it into the wastepaper basket with a shrug.

"Report-fever!" he would say to himself with a smile. "All officials get it in the harmattan. They write about everything to everybody; it means nothing."

There was one person at the station who never pronounced the word cerebrospinal, and that was the magistrate. His mind was full of Urgèle. While the others lost no opportunity to exchange sharp words, Flavien, his work finished, shut himself up in the prison he had chosen for himself weeks ago: his terrace. Only his boys were subjected to his raw nerves. Wandering near the courthouse one day I saw him slumped in a wooden chair. He had not shaved for some days and his shorts did not seem to me as white as they might have been. He turned his eyes in my direction but I was sure he didn't see me. He was smoking; the gray swirls, no doubt, were forming in the burning air the image of Urgèle. Amedéwovoé appeared behind him.

"Are you still skulking about there?" roared the magistrate. "Never a moment's peace; always someone spying. Get out—do you hear me? Get out!"

It was noon and the magistrate had not put on his pith helmet. "Oh, put it on, Flavien!" I begged silently. "Put it on, or you really will go quite mad."

"But it's the administrative mail, sir," persisted Amedéwovoé with a sideways look.

"Well, what of it? Get out."

As the boy lingered Flavien seized his glass of whisky and flung it in his face. This man, so apathetic a moment before, was now behaving like a very demon, addressing to Amedéwovoé and all humanity the foulest oaths.

White witch! This was what you had made of Flavien. In the days when he loved simply my body he was almost happy; there were times when he even laughed. I was his refuge. Now he knew only loneliness and bewilderment, exasperation and empty violence. At the Mission the Sisters had made me learn by heart the words of a saint: "Whoso attaches himself to that which is lost, is lost!" I should have liked to repeat those words to Flavien, to snatch him from despair. But at that moment I dared not walk up the steps of his house; it would have been the whisky bottle itself, not the glass, that I should have had flung in my face.

So I returned to the maternity clinic. As I reached the hospital I heard the ex-nun offering Capitaine Docteur her services.

"I know you're an excellent nurse," answered Frantz, "but I don't think we shall have to ask for your help here. We shall nip the epidemic in the bud. Five cases is not too bad, and there have been no new ones for two days. I don't understand why there's such a panic in the station. But you must excuse me, Madame Lambert, I have to get back to my wife."

"She's not ill, I hope?" she asked, with lively interest. "I've not seen her about Manoho for a long time."

She was no doubt thinking, her curiosity thoroughly aroused, "The couple we saw everywhere together have vanished separately. Something must have happened."

"Not ill, exactly," replied the doctor in a worried voice. "She feels very tired and eats nothing. She seems to be losing strength daily. If I wasn't ready to leave for France myself I wouldn't hesitate to send her home."

"You mustn't worry yourself, Doctor. Who doesn't feel exhausted just now? It's the harmattan."

He made no answer and heavily climbed the steps of his house without asking her in. She stood undecided, watching his massive, slightly stooping figure, and was on the point of turning away when she spied Urgèle, framed by a window. But was it really Urgèle? Not so long ago Urgèle had had a flowerlike complexion and fair hair arranged like a halo; she wore black dresses of ankle length, or spreading in billows of tulle; her face then revealed exaltation—a secret intensity. But this dim figure beneath the *seko* seemed half erased: the clear outlines, the color, the very life, were gone.

The face of the ex-nun betrayed her amazement.

"What has happened to Urgèle? She's very ill—she's dying!"

She had tended enough men and women in her life to recognize the signs of the great departure. I saw her walk slowly away, and felt in her a sudden and unexplained pity for this woman of whom she had spoken so much evil.

"I should like to help her," she may have thought. "To save her. But would she let me? And should I know what to say?"

It was Madame Docteur's destiny to touch the hearts of those about her. They felt a need to protect her from unseen foes. But she was too ethereally remote to be taken by the arm and addressed in a few simple words. People felt afraid of her without knowing why. So they left her alone and kept away, leaving her shut up in her isolation. Did she guess at these wilted impulses, these outstretched hands that fell away, these hopes that faded before they flowered?

That night I was sleeping on my mat at the clinic when the sense of someone beside me woke me with a start.

"Océa!" I stammered. "How did you get here? You're not allowed to go about alone."

I saw her shaven head gleaming in the moonlight. A dark robe that covered her from head to foot hid her novice's clothes.

"Sh!" she said. "Don't light the lamp. I came because I had to, but no one must know. I paid a lot of money to a driver to bring me here and to take me back secretly, before the first cockcrow."

Her blanket fell open as she sat down on the mat beside me, and I saw that she had been tattooed beneath the ribs in front, and also on her back.

"Océa, those scars are inflamed and nowhere near healing. People have been hurting you, haven't they?"

"They drew patterns on my skin with a bit of broken bottle and covered the cuts with black powder. I cried and screamed but they said the fetish would be angry if I didn't undergo the trial willingly. So then I was quiet."

My heart was thumping; that Océa had risked escaping to see me meant that something was very wrong. She had been running, as I could hear from her rapid breathing. Or was she just upset? No sound reached us from Capitaine Docteur's bungalow; only the seas along the bar roared rhythmically, pitilessly.

"And Fossou?" I asked suddenly.

"That's what I've come about, Doéllé! I love him and I haven't missed seeing him for a single night."

"What? Do you mean he comes to you in the convent? What are you saying, Océa?"

"It's no secret to the novices. Nearly all of us have reached maturity and our lovers come to us when the old priestesses are asleep. They can get through a brushwood fence that's a continuation of the convent wall. Some of them are fetishers from another convent."

"But I thought all novices, whether boys or girls, were sworn to chastity?"

"Agbatakbato would be mad with fury if he knew. He thinks we sleep peacefully all night, or if we can't sleep that we recite *Hebiesso* poems. He gave forty lashes to a novice whom he caught outside the sacred precincts, and next day he came to tell us with a terrible look in his eyes that if any girl brought scandal on the cult house he would kill her."

"Oh, be careful, Océa! You've been very rash, and

Agbatakbato never trifles with fetish laws. He'd stop at nothing if he found you, the pearl of the cloister, in Fossou's arms."

"Oh, Doéllé, but that's not all I have to tell you! I'm afraid I'm going to have a child!"

"Océa! You're not sure of that—say you're not sure!"

I had taken my sister's arm and now shook it roughly. A pregnant novice would be a sensation indeed. By taking careful precautions and distributing money and presents it is possible to arrange meetings with one's lover, but a pregnancy cannot be concealed for long. As soon as he knew of it Agbatakbato would cause the culprit to vanish, so as to avoid bringing the cult house into disrepute.

"Do you realize the risk you're running, Océa?" I asked, trembling in every limb.

"Yes, I do. That's why I came to you. You're so clever—you know so much—you must be able to help me. Give me some drink of herbs to free me from this terror. I'm so young—I haven't tasted life yet, Doéllé! I'll put up with being a fetisher, but I don't want to die."

Her voice quavered in fear, and down her thinning cheeks the tears were running. Her outer garment had slipped down on the mat and above the unbleached cotton of the novice's dress the moon lit up the swollen tattoo marks.

"I don't know of any herbal drink," I said slowly.

"The white people must have drugs," Océa insisted, clutching my cloth. "Ask Capitaine Docteur. Go and wake him up now and tell him what's happened to me. He'll help me, I'm sure—he can't let me die."

"Have you gone mad? Let a white man into a secret like that? Listen, Océa, go back to the convent. Tomorrow I'll find an African doctor and tell him about you. Next time you come and see me I shall be able to help you, I hope."

"Next time? There won't be any next time. It was all I could do to get out tonight, and I shall never be able to manage it again. If you don't help me now I'm lost."

"Do please calm yourself, Océa. It'll be several months before anyone will notice, and meanwhile I shall have time to help you."

"You forget that every month the fetish priestesses examine us closely. The old *Sossi* whom you saw at the fountain has been specially told to watch me, as soon as she notices anything abnormal she'll tell Agbatakbato, then a midwife will come and examine me and then . . . The good name of the sect must come first; there'll be no pity shown. They won't hesitate to kill me to save the *Vodoun*'s honor. Can't you do anything for me now, Doéllé?"

"Nothing, Océa. You can see, everyone's asleep here —whites, blacks, and mulattoes. Tomorrow, I promise you—"

"Then good-by, Doéllé!"

She left me, running—a light shade wrapped in a robe the color of night—a small, tearful victim submissive to her destiny. I was never to see her again alive.

"Océa! Wait a moment—listen!" I dashed out under the coconut palms, but she had already disappeared.

Remorse seized me for having let her go without better comfort. I could have hidden her, helped her to cross the border into the Gold Coast. I could have. . . . But we brood too long over tardy decisions and our good actions remain most often undone. Only when it's too late are we scorched by words we never spoke, and know the despair of attempts abandoned. . . .

Some days later Amérique told me that the *Hebiesso* novices were to appear in public at a great ceremonial gathering, and that Océa would perform her first ritual dance in the public place in Waji. I asked leave of Capitaine Docteur, who was the more willing to grant it as meningitis was decreasing among us in the south. I made all haste to the scene of the festival. Agbatakbato, draped in a white cloth, with burning eyes and raised chin, stood erect beside the drums awaiting the arrival of his novices, and I wondered, "Does he know already? Does he know that Océa is pregnant? Oh God of the Missions! If you really exist, protect Océa—she who is so gentle and so lovely!"

The priestesses of the sea, wearing tall, glistening hats, danced first. Then came the alligator fetishers with their little white caps; and those of the smallpox hung with cowrie shells, and with flashing sheets of micalike mirrors. One woman sent the crowd into transports of delight: her brown-paper costume aped that of soldiers, she waved a stick instead of a rifle and a torn old straw boater served as *chéchia*, the French colonial uniform cap. To the sound of the drums she mimicked a military march and the onlookers slapped their thighs and laughed. "It's an Avrékété fetisher—Avrékété the clown!"

But what did I care for any of these priestesses, or for the men in the gaudy colored skirts who sprang yelling into the ring, leaping like wild beasts and rolling their eyes? It was Océa I came to see—the hunted gaze of Océa that I must catch.

"I'll speak to her somehow, even at the risk of another scandal. I'll make her understand that I can save her and give her back her carefree youth. She must escape tonight. I've arranged her journey to the Gold Coast where Fossou can join her and where she can await her baby undisturbed."

Such were my excited thoughts.

Suddenly a ripple ran through the onlookers and all eyes turned toward the *Hebiesso* cult house. Preceded by a troop of black pigs the novices emerged in single file and moved solemnly toward the dancing place; with heads bent, bodies gleaming with oil, and hips bound in white cotton cloth, they looked the very image of purity and renunciation. I could not help smiling to reflect how these apparently inaccessible vestals met their lovers every night in the shadow of their convent, all unsuspected by the cruel Agbatakbato.

But my heart stopped; among these young shaven crowns I did not see that of Océa. The novices were now moving around the sacred tree and Océa was not there. I rubbed my eyes, hoping that this was a bad

dream and that I should suddenly spy my sister dancing
with the other girls the ritual dance of *Hebiesso*. Alas,
I was not dreaming. Fossou who was in the crowd
craned his neck desperately in search of his beloved,
and rolled his eyes in consternation. I went up to him.

"Where is she?" I whispered.

But he made no answer; against all hope he went on
seeking Océa among the white-robed novices. Agbatakbato surveyed their dancing with satisfaction; his expression changed only at some faulty movement which he
would be careful to punish severely on their return to
the cult house. The onlookers clapped their hands with
enthusiasm. How alone we felt, Fossou and I, with our
dread! And suddenly among the men and women assembled there, all seemingly bent on pleasure alone, the
murmur ran, "Océa's not among the novices—Océa's
not here!"

The voices grew louder, half curious, half uneasy:
"Why isn't Océa dancing with the others?"

An old woman approached me. "Your sister's not ill?
I saw her yesterday with the others at the fountain."

"Where is she, where is she?" they asked; and from
mouth to mouth the question rebounded like a ball:
"Where is she? Where is she?"

Seemingly indifferent to the noises of the crowd, the
novices went on dancing, in postures of humility. Agbatakbato, his chin lifted as usual, ostentatiously ignored
the excitement among the bystanders. A fetish priestess
I knew glided near me and whispered quickly, "Océa

was taken away last night. It seems she was with child and Agbatakbato was furious; he sent her away to another convent."

"Where? Which one? Tell me, please—please!"

"I don't know."

And she slipped quickly into the dancing circle.

The sun was setting. Under the watchful gaze of the priest the novices returned to their convent, while the drums resounded yet more loudly. The smallpox fetishers resumed their dancing, but these were no longer fervent dances of prayer. Holding one another by the neck or the waist they now mimicked the act of love, feigning voluptuous spasms and assuming the most lascivious postures, while children all about them clapped their hands and laughed. Night fell over the ground, and through it the teeth and eyes of the frenzied dancers gleamed luminously. Fossou and I moved away without a word, bowed down with grief.

In the market, women were already lighting candles and crouching silently before saucers of red beads, heaps of pimento, and smoked mudfish. Crickets struck up their strident song.

"Fossou!" I cried suddenly, "we must not give way to sorrow. We must find Océa. She's somewhere, God knows where, in danger of death. It would do no good to ask Agbatakbato; he'd say that Océa had run away and that he doesn't know where she's hiding. The other fetishers will be just as reticent. I shall go to the white people. I shall go now, at once, to the D.O. in Manoho, explain to him about Océa's disappearance and beg him to help us."

At that moment an old woman came out of the shadows, her hands pressed against her mouth to stifle a cry. It was my mother, and she had heard everything. Despite my stammered words of hope she sank into my arms, sobbing.

"Océa eyi Mawu me! I know—I know that Océa has gone to heaven!"

13

Elâ ke le du ji a fô na ke mlô amyi'a.

(The running beast wakens the sleeping
one.)

IN THE cassava planter's dining room a crab spider
was slowly climbing the wall behind the icebox that
occupied the place of honor on a platform. The punkah
swung above the hors-d'oeuvres.

"Doéllé came to see me last night," the D.O. was telling the magistrate. "Her young sister seems to have disappeared from a cult house in mysterious circumstances.
Indeed, I forwarded the complaint to you this morning."

"Yes, I read it," replied Flavien shortly.

"When can you begin the inquiry? Doéllé begged me
to act quickly. She seemed extremely worried."

213

"I shall start interrogating this afternoon. But we can't expect quick results. When did we ever get accurate or useful information from a fetisher? The case will probably be filed, for lack of proof."

"You know what an imagination the girl has, Flavien. She's convinced that her sister's been done away with."

"Need we pay much attention to Doéllé's notions? I think it's most unlikely to be a question of murder. Girls here are constantly disappearing and then come strolling back after a few days. I know that this is rather a special case and that Océa being both a novice and pregnant is in a very awkward situation. But as a rule novices arrange for an abortion, to avoid scandal. I did know of one who was thrown out of the cult house by the priest with the most humiliating ceremonies, but to do away with a girl is a very different thing. No, believe me, natives don't make such free use of poison as they did fifty years ago."

"Don't talk shop!" came old Lambert's resonant voice. "When people come to lunch with me it's for food, not for business. What do you think of this Australian butter? Ah, but it's not so good as the salt butter I made in Senegal when I caught a sea cow at the mouth of the Salé Saloum, with her breasts full of milk."

No one echoed his roar of laughter.

This lunch was to celebrate the withdrawal northward of the cerebrospinal epidemic—its shameful retreat to the starting point. It was the first meal shared by all the white colony since the beginning of the harmattan, and those invited, although reluctant, felt constrained to attend. Yet around these tense, tired people the air was still charged and sultry. Madame Commandant alone was absent; now that the threat of epidemic was past, now that she no longer felt constrained to make vigorous use of chlorinated pastilles and the gomenol syringe, she had relapsed and lacked the strength to walk up a dozen steps. Yet Madame Docteur, far weaker, had put on her violet dress, braided her hair about her head and taken her place between the D.O. and the agricultural officer. She had turned a deaf ear to Capitaine Docteur's expostulations: she wanted to see Flavien again. Since that last, desperate evening together at the resthouse—the evening when the python barred their road—she had not spoken to him. And she had to know whether his eyes were still gray, still ardent and pitiless by turns; whether the lines at the corners of his bitter mouth had deepened since their separation, and whether the scars of his old burns still showed as appealingly at his open shirt collar.

Everyone there felt a tightening of the throat at the sight of this silent, ethereal guest, who looked as if at any moment she might dissolve and fade away into thin air. The ex-nun felt an impulse to stretch out her arms and hold Urgèle down to earth. And when the boy brought in a great fish surrounded by green lemons she spoke to Madame Docteur in the voice of one offering a present to a difficult, fussy child.

"This is a *capitaine!*" she said. "I chose it in the market specially for you. I so much want you to taste it. Look, just this little piece, to please me! Do you know, our boy regards this fish as a god! Other fish are very poor things in comparison, he thinks. When he brings me a sole from the market he calls it a lieutenant, and a mullet is a sergeant-major."

What did Urgèle care for sea cows, captains, lieutenants, or sergeant-majors? Her eyes clung to Flavien's across the table, as if in farewell. I had come to the house with some medicine for the planter and was able to watch them from a distance as they sat opposite one another, and yet so far apart.

"I'm looking at him," Urgèle was thinking. "I'm looking at him and he's already lost to me. Most people when the time comes to part can fool themselves with words. 'See you soon,' they say. And they vow to write often and wait faithfully—we all say these things to help us hope against wind and tide. But to you I must say, 'Never again, Flavien, never again. . . .'"

The magistrate's knee moved beneath the table. I pictured Urgèle and Flavien as they had been at Christmas, with the same rolling surf on the bar. . . . In the black dress that clung to her like a second skin she had been haughty and beautiful, holding in her open hands all hopes, all dreams. And he, though he had never set eyes on her before, had recognized her at once: she was the woman he had been seeking for years, through deserts and forests, in nightly torment and the brightness of day. And he surveyed her with his narrowed eye, uttering a secret command; he shouted silently: "I've been waiting for you too long, Urgèle, for you to get away from me now. You shan't escape."

Yes, I well remembered the evening they had first

216

met. But Urgèle had not obeyed him: she had slipped away like water through his fingers. The punkah was still swinging above the table and the white people went on talking about fish as if they had been the most interesting creatures in the world.

"In the New Hebrides," the D.O. was saying, "everyone has his own boat. I went fishing there one day with a hook baited with a whole bullock's head, horns and all. It was swallowed by a huge shark, which turned out to have fifty-two young in its belly, all alive. They looked terrifying already."

Urgèle was thinking, "What is this weariness that makes me long for death? Holding a fork tires me, and lifting a glass is beyond my strength. The murmur of the surf is like a ceaseless wind in my ears and these people's faces hurt me. . . . I should like just to let my eyes slide over theirs, and chat to them casually; but something compels me to penetrate into them, to guess their thoughts and share in their troubles. I see the blood flowing in their veins, and their brains pulsate before my eyes, their nerves quiver naked. All their fears, regrets, and doubts beat against my heart and hurt it. I seem, without willing it, to be carrying all the cares of others. And Flavien whom I now look at and who looks so piercingly at me—fills me with weariness and dread too! If I had the strength I could leave Frantz and marry that man, whom perhaps I love. But the mere thought of the difficulties of such a step—the commonplace details— weigh me down. I'm afraid of unknown things—of words unspoken. Could Flavien love me as much if I became really ill and seemed to him to lose my looks? And who is he? I know nothing of his tastes or his deepest desires. We've never had time to talk, and I don't even know what sort of a little boy he was. I daren't leave Frantz, who's like my daily bread, and run off with this stranger."

The rest were still talking about fish. The agricultural officer let his colorless voice trickle on: "In Tahiti my wife gave us raw fish. She cut up a tunny into small pieces, soaked it in salt water, drained it, and covered it with the juice of green lemons. Then she sprinkled it with coconut milk and served it with sweet potatoes, yams, and baked bananas. It was delicious. You should try that recipe, ladies! Of course the Tahitian bananas have a particularly delicious flavor—"

"The Tahitian bananas, the Tahitian breadfruit, sunsets, guitars, vahines—! By harping on them all these months you've made us sick of the sound of South Sea Islands!" screamed Madame Elisabeth suddenly. And she burst into tears.

No one seemed startled by this outburst. Since the beginning of the harmattan no one had made any attempt to curb his or her remarks and had given way to nerves without causing any comment; as a result, anger lost its power and insults their venom.

"It's the harmattan!" they said with a shrug. "This is the 'Sudanitis' season. The rains will soon be here now."

Even the schoolmaster's little daughter was careful not to ask questions or fidget in her usual manner; she made herself small, she crouched like a timid little animal, waiting for the rains to bring peace again to Manoho.

So, during Madame Elisabeth's fit of weeping, everyone was silent, thinking of his own affairs. Old Lambert, knitting his white, bushy brows, reflected that the tapioca market had gone down decidedly since the arrival in France of cassava from Madagascar. The ex-nun imagined herself in her white wimple once more. Capitaine Docteur was silently reviewing the illnesses that might have caused this severe anemia in his wife, and raising his eyes saw that she was growing paler from moment to moment.

"Urgèle!"

She had fallen across the table, her head among the frangipani decorations on the cloth. Capitaine Docteur sprang to her side and helped by the former sister of mercy carried her into an adjoining room. Silence fell once more over the dining room.

"But what the devil's the matter with you all, with your white faces and your swoons?" thundered the cassava planter. "This isn't your first harmattan! Look at me—seventy, and fresh as a daisy. *Trompe-la-Mort*, they call me."

"Yes, yes, we know!" cried the exasperated Flavien, rising. "Right hand eaten by a cannibal, and the left by gangrene. And yellow fever and sleeping sickness. We know it all."

"Ah no, you don't! You never heard what happened to me at Bassiri, during the smallpox epidemic, when my car fell into the Sio. I managed to open the door and get to the surface, but I wasn't very handsome to look at.

219

The M.O. daubed me with iodine and wrapped me up like a mummy, and pushed me into bed at the dispensary. Opposite me there was another bed with a white man in it—except that he was more green than white. Well, you know my weakness: I enjoy conversation. 'What's wrong with you?' I asked him, but he never so much as flickered an eyelid to show he'd heard me. 'Well, what? Amoebic dysentery, hemorrhoids, snakebite?' I ran through all the diseases and accidents I could think of, and at the words 'blackwater fever' he gave a nod. Then I asked where he came from: 'Belgium, Czechoslovakia, Brazil, Switzerland?' and at that he nodded again. 'Trade? Photographer, provision merchant, piano tuner, journalist?' Yes, it was that—he moved his eyelashes. I went to sleep then, feeling pleased to have discovered something about the fellow. Next morning he was gone. 'Conked out, has he?' I asked the M.O. 'No,' he said, 'but you made him talk so much he's in a raging fever and I've had to isolate him.' What do you think of that—eh, Doctor?''

But Capitaine Docteur, who had reappeared supporting Urgèle on his arm, took his leave. Flavien was choking with rage because he had not the right to lean Urgèle against his shoulder and help her to walk. He was compelled to stay behind like a stranger, without even betraying his anxiety. As soon as the medical truck had left he was obliged to sit down again with the others, to smoke and accept a cup of coffee, and go on talking in an even voice about trivial things. Why was it not he who at this moment was helping Urgèle to undress—handing her the thermometer and the hot citronella? He could so well have comforted her. He would have said, "You'll soon be better, dear heart. But let me be selfish and enjoy seeing you lie there; you belong to me more, somehow. When you were well and in all your beauty you frightened me a little. Like this you seem nearer to me."

But Flavien knew that he couldn't even pay her a courtesy visit. Capitaine Docteur had forbidden him the house since their return from the north. More waiting, more fear. Flavien longed to spend his days and nights tending Urgèle and watching her face for signs of the progress or slackening of this mysterious illness. He had to be content with brief bulletins and contradictory reports that went the rounds of the station.

"She's better," the cassava planter said one day.

"Well, *I* don't think so. I'm afraid nothing can save her. She won't see another rainy season," Madame Elisabeth prophesied in a hollow voice.

"She's paler than ever," said Madame Commandant, shaking her head.

"It's as if she had left this world already," said the former nun, telling imaginary beads.

"Well, she had no fever this morning, anyway. She asked for oranges and pawpaws. I'm sure she'll get better," declared the D.O. curtly.

"Who is right? Who knows, here in Manoho?" Flavien must have wondered anxiously. "Ah, if I could only see Urgèle for myself—just for a moment—I should be free of this agonizing uncertainty. I should know at once. . . . They can all see Urgèle and speak to her, yet they can't even read her fate in her eyes!"

14

Koklotsu bé: vovo enyé agbé.

(Crows the cock: "Fear is life!")

"THE doctor's worried," said the agricultural officer one day. "He can't find out what's wrong with his wife, and he's called in two other doctors from Tocono."

I saw them come in a splendid gray car, a town car. They wore uniforms and gesticulated a great deal. I knew one of them, the Colonel, having worked for him for a fortnight or so on my return from Dakar. I ran to say good morning.

"Hullo, Doéllé!" he said. "Where are you working now—at the hospital or the maternity clinic? Do you know why the Captain sent for me? It seems his wife is ill."

"Yes, sir, she's very ill, but I don't know what's the matter with her."

"Well, we're going to find out," he answered, looking at me fixedly. I was disconcerted by this scrutiny—but why? I knew that the Colonel looked at everyone like that; it was a habit that had impressed me in Tocono when I worked with him. I never stopped trembling throughout the consultation. I twisted my hands, I snapped at Amavi the second nurse, and never took my eyes from the bungalow. A colonel is a man who knows; a man who has acquired more knowledge even than Capitaine Docteur. Suppose he were to find out the true cause of Urgèle's illness?

But at last the two doctors came down the steps and Capitaine Docteur walked with them to the gray car.

"I can find nothing specifically wrong," said the Colonel in a tone of authority. "She's very anemic and depressed. There's only one thing to be done and that's to send her home. I'll make out the certificate at once."

"But, sir," replied Capitaine Docteur, "you saw for yourself that Urgèle is in no fit state to travel. I think it might be better to wait a little. I expect my relief at any time now, and we'll sail as soon as she's able to stand on her feet."

"Well, Captain, in that case, since you meant to ignore my advice, you need scarcely have been in such a hurry to bring me out here."

And without heeding Capitaine Docteur's vague apologies the Colonel dived into the car, followed by the second doctor who had not spoken a word.

All that day the white people filed past Urgèle's bedside, before my eyes. White people hurt each other sometimes and say terrible things, but as soon as one of them falls ill they forget their quarrels. The mutual loyalty within their isolated little group, usually dormant, is sharply roused at a time like this, to form a shield about a threatened white life. In an instant the selfishness of the men and the pettiness of the women give place to devotion, outstretched hands, and unbounded generosity.

Cruelly jealous of Urgèle though she was, Madame Elisabeth offered to sit up with her all night. Madame Commandant left her bed to come and knit for whole afternoons beside someone more ill than herself. The ex-nun drove into Tocono to buy Vichy water for the woman she had so long despised. The desire aroused by Urgèle in the D.O., the agricultural officer, the schoolmaster, and the planter was swiftly transmuted into tenderness.

I watched them all hastening to her, one after the other, with anxious faces and hands full of presents. Only Flavien did not come; he had not the right. His boy Amedéwovoé went to inquire formally every morning, carrying a bunch of flowers. Slipping into the maternity clinic afterward he told me in a low voice, "The magistrate never used to care about his garden. Now he waters it every evening and he's forbidden me to touch the flowers; he wants to pick them himself. Isn't it strange, Doéllé?"

The boy's eyes creased mischievously and he put his

hand on his mouth to stifle a laugh. Naturally he couldn't understand. Those daily bunches of flowers were the only link between Urgèle and Flavien. Frail, ephemeral link perhaps, but one that allowed him to hope and to feel that his love was not lost forever.

Flavien had never been sentimental, and yet now, shy and stammering like a boy of sixteen, he charged his flowers with messages and prayers: "Tell Urgèle that I can't live without her. To hell with common sense! Let her get well quickly, then we'll surmount all obstacles together and never look back."

But Urgèle was far too exhausted to give ear to these impassioned murmurs. Laid on her bed the flowers looked like any other tropical bouquet and she waved away their oppressive fragrance.

"When I first came to Manoho," she told Capitaine Docteur, "I thought nothing could be lovelier than a spray of frangipani. But now I long for yellow and brown wallflowers—the ones that grow along lime-washed brick walls. I should like to pull the petals of peonies for the great summer procession. I think of the apricot trees and the sweet sap that oozes from them. . . ."

And Yaya who reported these words to me had difficulty in pronouncing the names of the flowers that Urgèle spoke of: phloxes, cornflowers, love-in-the-mist, bleeding heart. Words that set me dreaming.

"You shall taste apricot sap this summer," Capitaine Docteur is said to have replied, turning away his eyes, "and you shall see bleeding hearts in country gardens."

And lest he show himself too deeply moved—lest he say too much, and lie—Capitaine Docteur went quickly down to the hospital. Its walls, eaten by the dampness —that incurable leprosy—were his refuge. Bent over his microscope or his patients, Frantz found a measure of tranquillity. Through the windows he could see the families of the patients camping on the beach in a picturesque confusion of drying blankets, straying black pigs, and fires lit upon the sand. The tumult in his mind dispersed in slow and ever lessening waves.

On that day I watched for Capitaine Docteur to escape as usual to his work, for I had made up my mind to visit Urgèle and I had to be alone with her. Was it curiosity that impelled me to her bedside? Some morbid attraction, or simply the admiration that I had never ceased to feel for my rival? I did not know, but my heart thumped as I walked up the steps of her house with a few hibiscus flowers in my hand.

I had chosen my time carefully. No visitor disturbed the silence of the veranda. As in former days Amalia still sewed impassively; she was making bags for the coffee that was to be sent to France, and between two snips of the scissors she would lean on her elbows and stare at the lagoon. In the dining room the Child of the Moon was sweeping, bending over his short broom. Nothing was changed. I stood motionless at the top of the steps and seemed to hear voices from the past:

"Her name is Doéllé," Capitaine Docteur was saying. "She's about your age and I think you'll be seeing a lot

227

of her. She'll tell you endless stories about fetishes, poisonings and the blood pact. Doéllé's an expert in everything to do with her country; I'm always telling her she should write a book—aren't I, Doéllé?"

I remembered. . . . We had smiled then. And Kankwe ran up the coconut tree like a monkey. Everything was pleasant in those days—everything was clear and candid. The days passed smoothly and uneventfully. I knew nothing of passion. Flavien had not met Urgèle. Océa led a carefree life in my mother's hut.

On this silent, deserted veranda I seemed to see again Madame Docteur standing by the *seko* and pointing to the great baobab: "What is that gray tree?"

"That's the sacred baobab," I had replied. "At night it puts on a white robe to go out and choose its dead."

Capitaine Docteur's voice, precise and comforting as it was then, rang in my ear—so close, so close to me: "One day you'll be asking for the coconut milk that you scorn today," he was saying laughingly to Urgèle.

A slight noise made me start. Kankwe, coming from the kitchen, had appeared at the end of the veranda carrying a glass of coconut milk on a tray. He saw me, looked surprised, and then smiled. The smile was loathsome to me; I could have killed him for it. Impulsively I sprang forward and with a swift movement upset his tray. The cook stared in amazement at the broken glass and the spilled milk, and then . . .

"I'm sorry, Kankwe!" I said. "I jogged your arm by mistake and made you drop the tray."

We were standing at the door of Madame Docteur's

228

room. I turned slowly and saw her. Disembodied—that was what she had become. And through me. No one could have taken her for a woman now. There were waves in her flowing hair; there was all the sea in her eyes. It was not that she was like a seagull now—she *was* one. Not a patient lying in bed, but a sea bird poised on the swell. And this motionless bird regarded me fixedly in a stare that penetrated to my very depths. I had not been able to endure Kankwe's smile, but Madame Docteur's gaze was a thousand times harder to bear. "Forgive me!" I longed to cry. "Forgive me! Let me nurse you and make you well again. Let everything be as it was on our first day."

But I couldn't utter a sound. Madame Docteur went on looking at me without moving; then she too smiled. A half-smile such as I had so often seen on Flavien's lips, wherein could be read at once loneliness, disbelief, sorrow, and a fine irony.

"So it's true?" the smile said. "You've had me poisoned. But after all, what difference does it make?"

She smiled gently, with no other movement, her sea-eyes fixed upon me. Kankwe's conspiratorial smile of a moment ago still scorched me, and with it all Flavien's smiles, mocking or cruel. I was encircled by mouths drawing nearer to one another—threatening.

I fled, distracted. On the floor of the veranda, at the very spot where the python had been killed, I seemed to see a spreading patch of blood.

I ran and ran, remorse and terror clinging to my heels. Behind the maternity clinic I made a cushion of dry

grass, thrust into it a branch of the tree named *chivi*—
the stifler—and murmured four times: "This cushion
cannot complain of the branch. The branch pierces it
and it submits without being able to complain. It will be
the same with Madame Docteur: she has guessed that
her poisoning is my doing, but she will not speak of it."

It was a form of conjuration that Amérique had lately
taught me; and because I was just then thinking hard
about him he appeared suddenly in front of the hospital.
He was getting out of a truck in his ceremonial clothes,
carrying a golden stick which he was careful not to
allow to touch the ground.

I understood at once. It was not for my sake that
Amérique had come; he had been sent as the king of
Waji's representative to inquire after the health of Madame Docteur. With slow steps he made for the surgery
where he knew he would find Capitaine Docteur. The
stick laid across his arms gave him the portentous air of
a devotee carrying holy relics. I saw him bow very low
as he conveyed the good wishes for Madame Docteur's
recovery with which the king had charged him.

He spoke in a soft, respectful voice, and no one could
have supposed that Urgèle's health, after which he so
courteously inquired, was something that he himself had
destroyed. Capitaine Docteur, who knew the native customs, held the gold rod in his hands throughout the
speech, but he was evidently thinking of other things.
At last the two men separated and I ran to my friend.

"Amérique! I can't sleep—I'm hardly alive. The
white people have been looking at me queerly these last

few days and I'm terrified. I'm going off my head. Every time I meet the Sisters I make the sign of the cross. At the sight of a policeman I want to hold out my wrists for the handcuffs, and the smallest crowd makes me suspect a riot. I'm not living, I tell you—I'm not living! Océa was chosen by the fetish and then taken from the cult house because the gods accuse me and are taking vengeance on me. . . . Amérique, is there still time? Tell Kankwe not to put any more poison in the coconut milk. Madame Docteur mustn't die!"

"You do seem to have gone off your head," answered Amérique. He spoke somewhat haughtily because he was carrying the king's gold stick. "If you were so fond of Madame Docteur you shouldn't have asked me to make a blood pact with her cook."

"I acted in a fit of madness. I've only just seen what a crime I've committed. Help me, Amérique!"

"You're always asking me for help, but in return all you do is make promises. Fix the day of our wedding!"

"This is no time to talk of that, Amérique. We'll think about it later."

"Later—always later. But when *you* want something it has to be done at once. By living so much among white people, Doéllé, you've caught their habits."

But at last Amérique yielded to my entreaties and went to have a word with the cook. My heart was a little lighter.

"Don't let it be too late," I repeated, in a sort of litany. "Madame Docteur mustn't die."

The sacred baobab heard my supplication and spared Urgèle's life, leaving her gasping and broken on the shore. That very night it donned its white robe and stalked through Manoho to find another victim. Its scraggy limbs pointed to Madame Commandant.

The District Officer's wife had had heart trouble for some years, but she died that night, from myocarditis. She awoke, her hands clasped over her breast, where the baobab stabbed her without pity. A cold sweat poured off her, and pins and needles ran along her left arm. She called her husband who was sleeping in the other twin bed.

"Luc, I don't know what's the matter with me, but I'm going to die."

What she felt most cruelly was this certainty of imminent death. The D.O., stumbling over his sandals that lay by the bed, lit the lamp and gave his wife a few drops of adrenalin, without reflecting that this might cause a rupture in the heart. Then he sent his boy to the hospital with all speed.

The murmur of the surf filled the night when Capitaine Docteur came to wake me.

"Get ready quickly, Doéllé. Madame Commandant is seriously ill and I shall need you."

By the light of a hurricane lamp we set off through the darkness. The Residency was quite near the hospital, and for those few minutes I seemed to have returned to the happy times when I accompanied Capitaine Docteur on his expeditions to the bush.

"This is probably the last time we shall make a night

call together," he said. "My relief has just arrived by air. I expect to hand over to him within the next three days so as to take the next boat from Tocono."

"I'm glad for your sake," I answered, doing my utmost to conceal my feelings. "Madame Docteur will soon get better in France."

When we arrived Madame Commandant had just vomited. Capitaine Docteur examined her and found lowered blood pressure and slight fever. No sooner was he in the presence of illness than he regained his calm, assured demeanor and his voice was serene and comforting. Once more as in former days I was filled with enthusiasm for my work.

"I'll give her morphine to relieve the pain," he told the D.O. "It'll be a long business. We shall have to wait six weeks before we know how it'll go. Whatever happens she must be kept absolutely still and be spared all excitement. Doéllé will stay with her tonight and I'll come back at seven in the morning."

I settled down in a chair near the bed. The rolling of the seas against the bar rose and diminished unceasingly until I felt like screaming. The D.O. paced up and down without uttering a word, and paused now and then to look at the bloodless face of his wife.

He was reflecting: "She was never happy with me. When we married she was gay, enchanting. We were both twenty-five and we set off for the colonies as if for the conquest of the world. But time has passed. She grew old while my heart stayed young; she became the familiar presence that one never even noticed. I paid no more attention to what she said than to the words of a child. 'We haven't had a winter in France for so long,' she used to say. 'Luc, do take your leave in January if you can.' I shrugged my shoulders at the idea of leaving a hot country to arrive in Bordeaux in a hard frost. But oh, if she gets better I'll give her all she wants—snow, log fires, oysters, turkey, and chestnuts. I'll even give her a fur coat; she's always wanted beaver. She shall put it on and we'll go to the mountains, to the Jura, and she can feast her eyes on snow!"

At dawn the sick woman seemed to fall asleep. I advised the D.O. to get some rest while I went and asked the boy to make some coffee. I'd hardly entered the kitchen before a strangled cry brought me running back. Madame Commandant was lying dead beside her bed.

No doubt she had opened her eyes and believing herself alone had been frightened and tried to rise. Before she could take a step she had collapsed.

So she left us as she had lived, modestly. No visits, no anxiety on her account, no medicines from Tocono or elsewhere, no fuss. Her death was like the brown and beige sweaters she loved to knit. A little brown and beige death, quite unspectacular. And I said to myself, "How is it that such dim people can dwell side by side with such sparkling ones?"

The funeral took place next day at five o'clock in the afternoon. A delegation of Africans moved into the cemetery playing a stylized chant on a tuba, while the pupils of the Mission Sisters sang a psalm: "If Thou,

Lord, shouldst mark iniquities, O Lord, who shall stand?"

With the exception of Urgèle all the white people were gathered about the open grave; notwithstanding the heat, they stood close-packed together like sheep before a storm. The rough, hastily made coffin was taking down into the sand a little of their blood, of their hearts. Madame Commandant had been of no interest to them while alive; she had been ill equipped to win sympathy or affection. But in this place the disappearance of a European, however insignificant, had a profound effect. At home there's no time to look at death face to face. There are cars, there are films, there are bright lights and elevators, ringing telephones, trains running God knows where, and people dashing about with one eye on their watches. But here, far from home, white people pause and think. . . .

"Eternal rest give to them, O Lord, and let perpetual light shine upon them!" sang the little Africans in their shrill voices. And the whites said to themselves: "Tomorrow it may be my turn. The others will gather as they've gathered today, and it will be for me."

I was looking at Flavien. It was the first time I had seen him face to face outdoors and in public since we broke with one another, and I was surprised to feel nothing. He was even thinner than usual, and his lined face betrayed inward turmoil and distress.

"He knows that Urgèle is sailing tomorrow," I thought, "and that she's lost to him forever. He hasn't a thought for the woman we're burying. This cemetery

235

reminds him only of a lovers' meeting; he sees himself wandering with Urgèle beneath whispering palms and feels her in his arms again, amid the falling coconuts that crash on broken tombs."

But his blind gaze suddenly focused on myself. Flavien looked at me as steadily as the Colonel and as piercingly as Urgèle, unmoving, and with the disturbing fixity I had felt in the eyes of white people for some days. I could not run away; I had to remain beside the grave with piously folded hands, listening to the priest's prayers and the schoolmaster's address. I lowered my eyes to the sand. A big praying mantis quite near me was climbing a spray of thorn, and to regain my composure I tried to concentrate upon it.

"It's very pretty: a lady with a slender waist. Her little mouth is painted red and her folded wings are cut from green tissue paper."

I raised my eyes and slid a furtive glance at Flavien, hoping that he would have averted his own gaze. But his narrowed eye was still upon me and fear ran over my skin like an army of black ants. He was a magistrate: he could have me arrested.

Suppose he were to interrupt the schoolmaster's oration by shouting, "Look, look all of you! You're wondering what illness Madame Docteur has—the strange anemia from which she nearly died. Wonder no longer! She was poisoned—slowly, skillfully poisoned. The culprit is among you—it is Doéllé!"

I seemed already to feel the horrified gaze of the priest and the Sisters—"We thought she was such a

236

good Christian!" I imagined the amazement and violence of the doctor. I felt the hatred of the whole station breaking over me like a monstrous wave.

Unable to control my trembling I stepped back into the shadow of a rosy Portuguese tomb, and in an effort to fix my distracted mind I began to think of Océa.

"Where is she? When will she come back? The white people have looked for her in vain. My brothers have made sacrifices to *Hebiesso* to appease his anger—in vain. They cut the throat of a ram and poured its blood mixed with oil on the fetish. They offered white cocks to *Hebiesso*, saying, 'They are unbound—bind them thyself and we will immolate them to thee.' But alas, these fowls instead of lying motionless tried to escape. My elder brother broke their wings and legs, saying to the fetish, 'Do the same to our enemies!' He threw the limp bodies into the courtyard; but even the positions in which they fell were ill-omened and sinister."

When next I raised my head I gave a sigh of relief. Flavien was looking at me no longer; he was staring again at the rustling palms and dreaming of his lost love.

"Océa, Océa!" I said silently, calmer now. "Where are you? Come back to us, I beg of you! Yesterday our mother consulted the oracle, the *fa*. Bokonon the augur sprinkled water over Afan saying, 'May the coolness of peace be in the house.' Then he poured out spirits: 'May thy drunkenness be fatal to our enemies!' Then he scattered on the ground kola nuts cut into quarters. But the disposition of them made Bokonon say in fear, 'It is useless to offer corn and palm oil to the fetish. He is

237

honest and refuses your gifts, for the future is too dark.'
And at this my mother wept bitterly."

The white people were now filing past the grave,
throwing a little sand on the coffin and moving slowly
away among the English epitaphs and tattered paper
garlands. I was preparing to follow the Sisters when a
little boy pulled me by the arm. His little black face was
alive with terror.

"Doéllé! Come! Come quickly—they've found
Océa."

15

Du be lâ du kakla ye ja n'a'e.

(Meat of the town is carved by a knife
of the town.)

SOME days had passed.

At the maternity clinic I was tending a Wachi
woman in labor. I had removed her blanket and amulets and was splashing her abdomen with cold water
while the midwife vigorously massaged her body. The
woman was delivered kneeling, and hardly was it over
when she rose and went to sit down in a corner, groaning slightly. I gave her a small glass of rum to revive her,
and went out.

Rain was falling heavily. The last tornado had
snapped the power lines, carried away the planter's
sheet-iron roof, and flattened a wall of the Python Tem-

239

ple. Rain was pouring into Madame Elisabeth's room, but the schoolmaster paid little heed to it. To colonials, furniture has only the value of usefulness, and no sentiment attaches to it. It endures drought and damp, sun and rain. Chairs, tables, and beds are sold to one's successors on leaving, and other impersonal chairs, tables, and beds are bought in the new station. These things resemble the forced friendships formed during a stay at Bamako or Kurussa: like them they last two years, and no more is expected of them.

Palm branches were waving about like mad arms. Bloodlike mud poured off the road, and the natives, lifting their blankets high, splashed one another with shouts of laughter. The rain fell steadily. And in this unleashing of higher forces the lagoon lay breathing, impassive, looking at me out of the corner of its eye like a crocodile.

"Look at me now, look at me!" it said ironically. "Look at me once more before you go."

But I did not want to look. The lagoon conjured up the worst memory of my life and I preferred to turn my back upon it.

"Come now, where's your courage?" it persisted in hateful mockery. "Tomorrow you'll be driving along the northern roads to take up work at your new post among the victims of sleeping sickness. You've finished with Manoho and the lagoon. Look at me for the last time."

And so my thoughts were forced back to the evening

when I found Océa. How shall I ever forget that scene? With a mat for raft, my sister floated upon the lagoon, her arms and legs outstretched in the attitude of victims sacrificed to the *Vodoun*. All about me resounded a horror-stricken clamor. Africans were running from the farthest huts, groaning and shrieking. In their eyes, a person dying tragically in time of peace must have committed some secret crime. They shook their fists at the floating mat. "She angered the fetish and the fetish has slain her!" they howled.

Unable to stir hand or foot I stared at Océa's emaciated body—at the skin that I had known, so satiny, so gleaming with cosmetics. I stared at the distorted mouth that I had so often seen laughing. I stared at the limp little hands and remembered how she had looked, walking beside me with her palms turned upward to the sun, offering their fingers like jewels.

I seemed to hear her childish voice as she dressed my hair in the Abongo manner: "Doéllé, I often dream that I'm setting off in a big pirogue on the lagoon. I stand up in the bows without friends or baggage; I don't know where I'm going, but I feel it's far away."

I hid my face in my hands.

"Océa, Océa my sister, you have died the death I meant for Urgèle. Océa—so young, so beautiful— you've paid the price of my vile intention."

And the people knew nothing of this; they even pitied me because I had lost my sister in so shameful a manner. For a moment, so keen was my pain and remorse, I longed to cry out to them, "Océa did nothing wrong! She was guilty of no treachery or false witness, no hidden crime such as you speak of. I am the culprit."

But it is seldom that one dares follow one's impulses. And what good would it have done to give myself up? Océa was dead. Even if they had stoned me or thrown me into prison she could not have been brought back. Therefore I uttered not a sound; and suddenly, strangely, the growing clamor around the lagoon died away. The waving coconut palms were stilled. The goats and the black pigs that had been careering panic-stricken about our feet disappeared as by magic, and in the sky terrifying black clouds were piling up. Silence had fallen: a silence that might have boded the end of the world. One could feel that dreadful forces, long pent up, were on the point of release.

"*Hebiesso* is very powerful!" bleated an old woman.

"Yes, yes—*Hebiesso* is very powerful!" echoed the crowd in a shout that shook the ground.

A grumbling roar rolled behind the clouds. In terror I flung myself down with all the others. I saw *Hebiesso* appear in the form of a fiery serpent, and in an unearthly voice he exhorted thunder and lightning to annihilate the world. Another zigzag flash, and the black sky opened to discharge its cataracts.

"Rain!" cried the people, lifting their hands in thankfulness.

"Rain!" said the white people with a sigh of relief.

"Rain!" I murmured, letting my arms fall to my sides. The black pigs tumbled from the huts, turning their parched snouts upward to the liquid rods. Dusty palm trees spattered themselves; dying plants came instantly to life. Water rushing over the ground made a brook of the least furrow and a waterfall of the smallest ledge. A thousand drums began to beat rhythmically on the hospital roof.

My companions, whom I had seen prostrated five minutes before, now gave noisy expression to their joy, stripping off their blankets to offer their naked bodies to the downpour.

I took advantage of the general jubilation to carry Océa's remains swiftly away. Two men I knew helped me. The driver of the Syrians' truck, who had so often taken me to Waji, consented to take charge of the slender little body and we set off through the pitiless rain.

"If only the fetishers don't claim her," I thought anxiously. "A novice who has died such a death might be dragged along by the hair to the sound of horns hung with human jawbones, and the villagers would want to spit on the corpse. Oh God, let Océa have decent burial!"

Let me not think of my mother's despair or of Fossou's cries when our mournful party drew up before the hut. No, I will not think of it again. I would rather remember Océa's friends who, heedless of the ban, brought food, blankets, and money for her great journey. They did not weep; they held fans of plaited straw and gently fanned the dead girl.

Now Océa lies in the ground with the presents that

these friends brought her, and my mother wanders along the riverbanks seeking her soul.

All is peace once more. But I cannot bear the sight of the lagoon. I would rather turn toward the bungalow where Capitaine Docteur lived for two years. A new white doctor goes by on his way to the hospital, and overhead a woman's heels tap the floor of the veranda. It's not Urgèle, how could it be? She sailed six days ago, from Tocono. This is the wife of the new doctor: a woman like the rest.

Today silence envelops those flimsy walls, once vibrant with passion. The weaverbirds are quiet and even the roar of the bar is muffled by rain. There is nothing around the house but rain. Rain washes out sorrow as India rubber effaces inkstains. Amalia, indifferent witness of the past, hems her cloths and leans on her elbows beneath the *seko;* the new Madame Docteur has taken her into her service. Amalia I am sure will handle her scissors and gaze at the lagoon until the end of time.

Now I say good-by to the midwives and to Amavi, the second nurse.

"Forgive me," I say to Amavi. "I was often harsh, but I was very fond of you. Don't let your memory of me be a bad one."

Over my robe I put on an old waterproof that Urgèle left behind, and walk away along the blood-colored road. The Child of the Moon, Bokari, and Kankwe the impenitent cook are sitting on a bench out of the rain, chattering and cackling; already jeering at their new masters. Their laughter follows me as I enter the drenched cemetery. The paper garlands have disintegrated in the rain, mounds crumble and the waters pour into the cracks of the stones. . . .

"Who sows the wind shall reap the whirlwind," murmurs a tomb as I pass. "Departed this Life to Life Eternal. Died of yellow fever. Died of yellow fever. *Auf Wiedersehen!*"

Doesn't Madame Commandant feel cold beneath the rain? The lightest breeze used to make her shiver. And you, Océa, buried in lime and therefore invisible among the dead—are you at this moment wandering between the flooded graves? Oh, I know you've forgiven me, and yet I'm frightened and keep turning my head as if I were being followed. At night I cry out in my dreams; I don't know whether it's the God of the Missions that rebukes me or the fetishes that brush my ear—my conscience weeping or the threats of the *Vodoun*.

I'm only an *évoluée;* I've come only halfway and I don't know the end of the road. I surrender by turns to certainty and doubt, to courage and cowardice. I tried everything, risked everything, to take Urgèle from Flavien. I betrayed Capitaine Docteur's trust, eluded Amérique, sacrificed Océa, and lost my soul. Yet when I had almost reached my goal I faltered and gave up. But of those I know, have any fulfilled their destinies? If Amérique had wholeheartedly desired to marry me he would not have been content with false promises. When he heard that I had applied for a transfer to the north he should have riveted my chains. But he went away without a word. Capitaine Docteur wanted to kill Urgèle with his hunting knife, yet he held his hand. If Urgèle had truly loved Flavien she would have left everything for his sake, without reflecting that she hardly knew him. If Flavien had wanted to keep Urgèle he would have leaped all obstacles, thrown down all barriers, and carried her off like a hero of ancient times.

I ask myself sorrowfully: "Must it be everyone's fate to vacillate like this, without ever finding certainty?"

Here I am at the courthouse. The rain has suddenly stopped. Leaves unfold quickly and sap runs along the branches. Mayflies murmur in their swarms and flying foxes flit about my wet hair, squeaking those shrill squeaks that Flavien could never endure. Voices come to me from the sitting room, and guided by them I move noiselessly forward. I see Flavien first; he stands before a big, shining wheeled table. Bottles are lined up before him in handsome array and the glasses sparkle. Nothing is lacking, neither limes nor icewater. He hands gin to Madame Elisabeth and smiles because the little girl pulls her mother's skirt, simpering affectedly, and asks for pineapple juice.

"Well, Madame Lambert, so you're going on leave?" Flavien remarks amiably, offering the planter's wife a cigarette.

"Yes, indeed," the ex-nun replies laughing. "In a fortnight we shall be drinking rich, creamy milk in the Alps. My family won't know me. The last time they saw me I was wearing the cornette, wasn't I, Lambert?"

"I want a drink!" roared the planter by way of answer, holding out his glass. "Give me a drink!"

246

"Cognac or whisky?" asks Flavien benignly, a bottle in each hand.

Amazed I rise on tiptoe and survey those relaxed faces, listen to their calm voices and think: "What? Have all those rages and explosions and tears given place so soon to this flatness and mediocrity? The harmattan set them at each other's throats, and now the rainy season has given them back their equable tempers. They seem to have forgotten everything: bitter words, Madame Commandant's death, Urgèle's strange beauty—none of these things ever existed. There they sit around the bar, watching the rain and drinking. Above all drinking. Africans, after the Epé-Ekpé celebrations, when friends want to make up their quarrels, drink together. "Water," they say, "quenches the fire of anger."

"Our next station will be Tahiti!" announces the schoolmaster. "It was you, *l'agriculteur*, who gave us the idea of going there, with all your tales of clear lagoons, ropes of flowers, and vahines. And Elisabeth can't wait to taste the raw fish you talked about." The schoolmaster gave a slight smile, without malice. "Perhaps the place isn't so bad after all. We shall see!"

The agricultural officer turned to the D.O. "Then I shall be the only one left of the old gang. It'll be all new blood here. You yourself, *monsieur l'administrateur*, are to take up more important work, I hear. And you, my dear Flavien, when are you off to Niamey?"

"In about three weeks."

I'm struck by the change in Flavien since the rains started. His cheeks are less hollow, his knee no longer quivers when he's seated. Before, his eye used to narrow in a disturbing manner, I remember; but today his look is tranquil and friendly. All the same, you're suffering, Flavien. It still hurts. It would be sad indeed if this were not so. Urgèle has gone. You heard the ship's siren bellowing good-by? And yet your heart seems the lighter for it. . . . I don't understand. I shall never understand the hearts of white people. Here they are all gathered at the courthouse and no one mentions Capitaine Docteur. No one says, "I wonder how little Urgèle will stand the voyage."

But I think of them unceasingly. I see Capitaine Docteur as he was a year ago in the rains. He was to perform an operation on a native in a remote village and took me with him. We had to drive through swamps and we got bogged down in the mud. Giant grasses hid the road from us. Bridges of boughs collapsed. Our pirogue capsized and we were thrown into the flooded river—we, the lamp, and the surgical equipment. When we arrived the waters had flooded the village and the inhabitants were mired to the thighs. But what mattered rain, mud, flood, and wet clothes? We were at peace. Capitaine Docteur could smoke his pipe without finding things to worry about, while the mere thought of Flavien made me laugh and sing. I remember that operation by the light of the storm lantern. We laid the man on a door that had been taken off its hinges. Rain leaked into the ramshackle hut on all sides, and yet Capitaine Docteur moved in this damp twilight with the same ease as if he'd been in the operating theater at Dakar. His white overall was stained with blood, and sweat was running down his forehead. The patient's dog barked savagely at us all through the operation and even tried to bite.

That is the best picture I have of him. Why remember the other times? It does no good. For me he will always be the bush surgeon, bending over a patient in the half-light of a wretched hut.

But Urgèle when I think of her has a hundred faces. Faces fleeting as the river, as the clouds—faces I cannot hold in my mind. She dabs her forehead with a little green handkerchief, throws back her hair, wears a black dress, a violet one, a tulle skirt, a negligee with wide white sleeves. She carries a bunch of red ixoras, she drinks a glass of coconut milk, she looks at me, and looks. . . . Then she slips away. Urgèle is no more than a pair of eyes the color of the sea, intense, unfathomable; eyes fixed upon me forever.

The rain is falling again. The white people are drinking and chatting. My blanket, notwithstanding the waterproof that covers it, is soaked. Yet, fascinated, I go on watching the remaining actors of this drama who, as in the theater, rise up after their feigned deaths and smile. Smile at one spectator: myself.

Myself, separated from them by a curtain of rain. Myself, the black facing the whites. Myself, the unseen onlooker, hidden now in the wings, now in the orchestra, now in the flies, now in the prompter's box; always secret, always present, with a heart seared from the lines spoken by the players.

But the kerosene lamp that illuminates the white people begins to flicker, faint, and fail. No one rises to turn up the flame; it sinks and dies. Darkness. And motionless the characters in my story melt into the night, into the rain. . . .

Free of them now, I walk away down the red road.

Soon I shall know other white people; another magistrate perhaps will love this skin of mine that is as soft as the wing of a flying fox. They will all smile at me, talk to me, and sometimes address me formally as Mademoiselle. Yet the politer they are the more they will be thinking: "You're only a Negress after all. Go back to your own people." And I shall answer softly, "I would gladly go to them—but where are they?"

Then they will look away, like the cassava planter, the District Officer, and Flavien. And I shall go on my way: a way without handrails, signposts, or notice boards to guide me.

The day will come when I shall marry a man of my own standing, some African doctor, perhaps. I shall have a son whom I will call Flavien in memory of an unhappy love. I shall send him to school in Tocono, and when he has won a scholarship he will finish his education in France. I can imagine his return, and dread it already. He will drive a gray car as shiny as the Colonel's and his casual air will seem to me a stranger's. He will bring out photographs of the Arc de Triomphe from his wallet, and boast continually of his life in Paris and his Parisian friends. And who knows . . . Perhaps I shall say to him: "Was your life there so splendid—your white friends so dear to you? Well then, my son, this is not the place for you. Go back to your own people!"